Henry James

Henry James OM (15 April 1843 – 28 February 1916) was an American-British author regarded as a key transitional figure between literary realism and literary modernism, and is considered by many to be among the greatest novelists in the English language. He was the son of Henry James Sr. and the brother of renowned philosopher and psychologist William James and diarist Alice James.

He is best known for a number of novels dealing with the social and marital interplay between émigré Americans, English people, and continental Europeans. Examples of such novels include The Portrait of a Lady, The Ambassadors, and The Wings of the Dove. His later works were increasingly experimental. In describing the internal states of mind and social dynamics of his characters, James often made use of a style in which ambiguous or contradictory motives and impressions were overlaid or juxtaposed in the discussion of a character's psyche.(Source: Wikipedia)

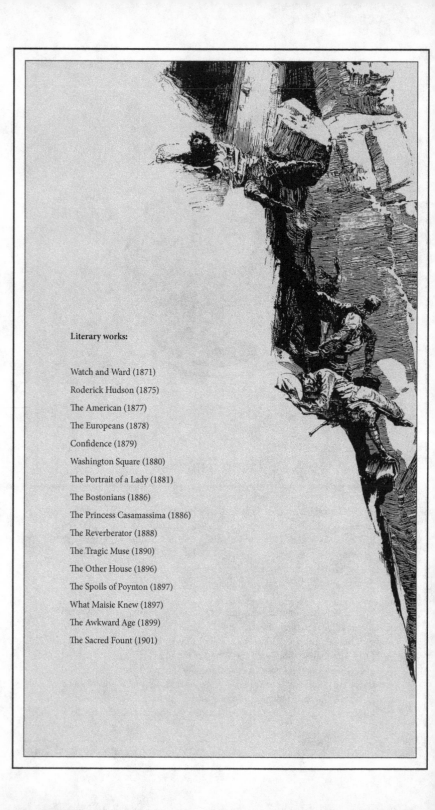

Literary works:

Watch and Ward (1871)

Roderick Hudson (1875)

The American (1877)

The Europeans (1878)

Confidence (1879)

Washington Square (1880)

The Portrait of a Lady (1881)

The Bostonians (1886)

The Princess Casamassima (1886)

The Reverberator (1888)

The Tragic Muse (1890)

The Other House (1896)

The Spoils of Poynton (1897)

What Maisie Knew (1897)

The Awkward Age (1899)

The Sacred Fount (1901)

THE
WORKS
OF
HENRY JAMES

VOL. 27 (OF 36)

THE MARRIAGES
THE MIDDLE YEARS

An Imprint of Moon Classics LLC

A Wholly Owned Subsidiary of Queenior LLC

A Melodragon Company

First Printing: 2020

ISBN 978-1-6627-1600-3 (Paperback)

ISBN 978-1-6627-1601-0 (Hardcover)

Published by Moon Classics

www.moonclassics.com

Contents

THE
WORKS
OF
HENRY JAMES
VOL. 27 (OF 36)

THE MARRIAGES

I

"WON'T you stay a little longer?" the hostess asked while she held the girl's hand and smiled. "It's too early for every one to go—it's too absurd." Mrs. Churchley inclined her head to one side and looked gracious; she flourished about her face, in a vaguely protecting sheltering way, an enormous fan of red feathers. Everything in her composition, for Adela Chart, was enormous. She had big eyes, big teeth, big shoulders, big hands, big rings and bracelets, big jewels of every sort and many of them. The train of her crimson dress was longer than any other; her house was huge; her drawing-room, especially now that the company had left it, looked vast, and it offered to the girl's eyes a collection of the largest sofas and chairs, pictures, mirrors, clocks, that she had ever beheld. Was Mrs. Churchley's fortune also large, to account for so many immensities? Of this Adela could know nothing, but it struck her, while she smiled sweetly back at their entertainer, that she had better try to find out. Mrs. Churchley had at least a high-hung carriage drawn by the tallest horses, and in the Row she was to be seen perched on a mighty hunter. She was high and extensive herself, though not exactly fat; her bones were big, her limbs were long, and her loud hurrying voice resembled the bell of a steamboat. While she spoke to his daughter she had the air of hiding from Colonel Chart, a little shyly, behind the wide ostrich fan. But Colonel Chart was not a man to be either ignored or eluded.

"Of course every one's going on to something else," he said. "I believe there are a lot of things to-night."

"And where are *you* going?" Mrs. Churchley asked, dropping her fan and turning her bright hard eyes on the Colonel.

"Oh I don't do that sort of thing!"—he used a tone of familiar resentment that fell with a certain effect on his daughter's ear. She saw in it that he thought Mrs. Churchley might have done him a little more justice. But what made the honest soul suppose her a person to look to for a perception of fine shades? Indeed the shade was one it might have been a little difficult to seize—the difference between "going on" and coming to a dinner of twenty people. The pair were in mourning; the second year had maintained it for Adela, but the Colonel hadn't objected to dining with Mrs. Churchley, any more than he had objected at Easter to going down to the Millwards', where he had met her and where the girl had her reasons for believing him to have known he should meet her. Adela wasn't clear about the occasion of their original meeting, to which a certain mystery attached. In Mrs. Churchley's exclamation now there was the fullest concurrence in Colonel Chart's idea; she didn't say "Ah yes, dear friend, I understand!" but this was the note of sympathy she plainly wished to sound. It immediately made Adela say to her "Surely you must be going on somewhere yourself."

"Yes, you must have a lot of places," the Colonel concurred, while his view of her shining raiment had an invidious directness. Adela could read the tacit implication: "You're not in sorrow, in desolation."

Mrs. Churchley turned away from her at this and just waited before answering. The red fan was up again, and this time it sheltered her from Adela. "I'll give everything up—for *you*," were the words that issued from behind it. "*Do* stay a little. I always think this is such a nice hour. One can really talk," Mrs. Churchley went on. The Colonel laughed; he said it wasn't fair. But their hostess pressed his daughter. "Do sit down; it's the only time to have any talk." The girl saw her father sit down, but she wandered away, turning her back and pretending to look at a picture. She was so far from agreeing with Mrs. Churchley that it was an hour she particularly disliked. She was conscious of the queerness, the shyness, in London, of the gregarious flight of guests after a dinner, the general *sauve qui peut* and panic fear of being left with the host and hostess. But personally she always felt the contagion, always conformed to the rush. Besides, she knew herself turn red now, flushed with a conviction that had come over her and that she wished not to show.

Her father sat down on one of the big sofas with Mrs. Churchley; fortunately he was also a person with a presence that could hold its own. Adela didn't care to sit and watch them while they made love, as she crudely imaged it, and she cared still less to join in their strange commerce. She wandered further away, went into another of the bright "handsome," rather nude rooms—they were like women dressed for a ball—where the displaced chairs, at awkward angles to each other, seemed to retain the attitudes of bored talkers. Her heart beat as she had seldom known it, but she continued to make a pretence of looking at the pictures on the walls and the ornaments on the tables, while she hoped that, as she preferred it, it would be also the course her father would like best. She hoped "awfully," as she would have said, that he wouldn't think her rude. She was a person of courage, and he was a kind, an intensely good-natured man; nevertheless she went in some fear of him. At home it had always been a religion with them to be nice to the people he liked. How, in the old days, her mother, her incomparable mother, so clever, so unerring, so perfect, how in the precious days her mother had practised that art! Oh her mother, her irrecoverable mother! One of the pictures she was looking at swam before her eyes. Mrs. Churchley, in the natural course, would have begun immediately to climb staircases. Adela could see the high bony shoulders and the long crimson tail and the universal coruscating nod wriggle their horribly practical way through the rest of the night. Therefore she *must* have had her reasons for detaining them. There were mothers who thought every one wanted to marry their eldest son, and the girl sought to be clear as to whether she herself belonged to the class of daughters who thought every one wanted to marry their father. Her companions left her alone; and though she didn't want to be near them it angered her that Mrs. Churchley didn't call her. That proved she was conscious of the situation. She would have called her, only Colonel Chart had perhaps dreadfully murmured "Don't, love, don't." This proved he also was conscious. The time was really not long—ten minutes at the most elapsed—when he cried out gaily, pleasantly, as if with a small jocular reproach, "I say, Adela, we must release this dear lady!" He spoke of course as if it had been Adela's fault that they lingered. When they took leave she gave Mrs. Churchley, without intention and without defiance, but from the simple sincerity of her pain, a longer look into the eyes than she had ever given her before. Mrs. Churchley's onyx pupils reflected the question as distant dark windows reflect the sunset; they seemed to say: "Yes, I *am*, if that's what you want to know!"

What made the case worse, what made the girl more sure, was the silence preserved by her companion in the brougham on their way home.

They rolled along in the June darkness from Prince's Gate to Seymour Street, each looking out of a window in conscious prudence; watching but not seeing the hurry of the London night, the flash of lamps, the quick roll on the wood of hansoms and other broughams. Adela had expected her father would say something about Mrs. Churchley; but when he said nothing it affected her, very oddly, still more as if he had spoken. In Seymour Street he asked the footman if Mr. Godfrey had come in, to which the servant replied that he had come in early and gone straight to his room. Adela had gathered as much, without saying so, from a lighted window on the second floor; but she contributed no remark to the question. At the foot of the stairs her father halted as if he had something on his mind; but what it amounted to seemed only the dry "Good-night" with which he presently ascended. It was the first time since her mother's death that he had bidden her good-night without kissing her. They were a kissing family, and after that dire event the habit had taken a fresh spring. She had left behind her such a general passion of regret that in kissing each other they felt themselves a little to be kissing her. Now, as, standing in the hall, with the stiff watching footman—she could have said to him angrily "Go away!"—planted near her, she looked with unspeakable pain at her father's back while he mounted, the effect was of his having withheld from another and a still more slighted cheek the touch of his lips.

He was going to his room, and after a moment she heard his door close. Then she said to the servant "Shut up the house"—she tried to do everything her mother had done, to be a little of what she had been, conscious only of falling woefully short—and took her own way upstairs. After she had reached her room she waited, listening, shaken by the apprehension that she should hear her father come out again and go up to Godfrey. He would go up to tell him, to have it over without delay, precisely because it would be so difficult. She asked herself indeed why he should tell Godfrey when he hadn't taken the occasion—their drive home being an occasion—to tell herself. However, she wanted no announcing, no telling; there was such a horrible clearness in her mind that what she now waited for was only to be sure her father wouldn't proceed as she had imagined. At the end of the minutes she saw this particular danger was over, upon which she came out and made her own way to her brother. Exactly what she wanted to say to him first, if their parent counted on the boy's greater indulgence, and before he could say anything, was: "Don't forgive him; don't, don't!"

He was to go up for an examination, poor lad, and during these weeks his lamp burned till the small hours. It was for the Foreign Office, and there was to be some frightful number of competitors; but Adela had great hopes of him—she believed so in his talents and saw with pity how hard he worked. This would have made her spare him, not trouble his night, his scanty rest, if anything less dreadful had been at stake. It was a blessing however that one could count on his coolness, young as he was—his bright good-looking discretion, the thing that already made him half a man of the world. Moreover he was the one who would care most. If Basil was the eldest son—he had as a matter of course gone into the army and was in India, on the staff, by good luck, of a governor-general—it was exactly this that would make him comparatively indifferent. His life was elsewhere, and his father and he had been in a measure military comrades, so that he would be deterred by a certain delicacy from protesting; he wouldn't have liked any such protest in an affair of *his*. Beatrice and Muriel would care, but they were too young to speak, and this was just why her own responsibility was so great.

Godfrey was in working-gear—shirt and trousers and slippers and a beautiful silk jacket. His room felt hot, though a window was open to the summer night; the lamp on the table shed its studious light over a formidable heap of text-books and papers, the bed moreover showing how he had flung himself down to think out a problem. As soon as she got in she began. "Father's going to marry Mrs. Churchley, you know."

She saw his poor pink face turn pale. "How do you know?"

"I've seen with my eyes. We've been dining there—we've just come home. He's in love with her. She's in love with *him*. They'll arrange it."

"Oh I say!" Godfrey exclaimed, incredulous.

"He will, he will, he will!" cried the girl; and with it she burst into tears.

Godfrey, who had a cigarette in his hand, lighted it at one of the candles on the mantelpiece as if he were embarrassed. As Adela, who had dropped into his armchair, continued to sob, he said after a moment: "He oughtn't to—he oughtn't to."

"Oh think of mamma—think of mamma!" she wailed almost louder than was safe.

"Yes, he ought to think of mamma." With which Godfrey looked at the tip of his cigarette.

"To such a woman as that—after *her*!"

"Dear old mamma!" said Godfrey while he smoked.

Adela rose again, drying her eyes. "It's like an insult to her; it's as if he denied her." Now that she spoke of it she felt herself rise to a height. "He rubs out at a stroke all the years of their happiness."

"They were awfully happy," Godfrey agreed.

"Think what she was—think how no one else will ever again be like her!" the girl went on.

"I suppose he's not very happy now," her brother vaguely contributed.

"Of course he isn't, any more than you and I are; and it's dreadful of him to want to be."

"Well, don't make yourself miserable till you're sure," the young man said.

But Adela showed him confidently that she *was* sure, from the way the pair had behaved together and from her father's attitude on the drive home. If Godfrey had been there he would have seen everything; it couldn't be explained, but he would have felt. When he asked at what moment the girl had first had her suspicion she replied that it had all come at once, that evening; or that at least she had had no conscious fear till then. There had been signs for two or three weeks, but she hadn't understood them—ever since the day Mrs. Churchley had dined in Seymour Street. Adela had on that occasion thought it odd her father should have wished to invite her, given the quiet way they were living; she was a person they knew so little. He had said something about her having been very civil to him, and that evening, already, she had guessed that he must have frequented their portentous guest herself more than there had been signs of. To-night it had come to her clearly that he would have called on her every day since the time of her dining with them; every afternoon about the hour he was ostensibly at his club. Mrs. Churchley *was* his club—she was for all the world just like one. At this Godfrey laughed; he wanted to know what his sister knew about clubs. She was slightly disappointed in his laugh, even wounded by it, but she knew perfectly what she meant: she meant that Mrs. Churchley was public and florid, promiscuous and mannish.

"Oh I daresay she's all right," he said as if he wanted to get on with his work. He looked at the clock on the mantel-shelf; he would have to put in another hour.

"All right to come and take darling mamma's place—to sit where *she* used to sit, to lay her horrible hands on *her* things?" Adela was appalled—all the more that she hadn't expected it—at her brother's apparent acceptance of such a prospect.

He coloured; there was something in her passionate piety that scorched him. She glared at him with tragic eyes—he might have profaned an altar. "Oh I mean that nothing will come of it."

"Not if we do our duty," said Adela. And then as he looked as if he hadn't an idea of what that could be: "You must speak to him—tell him how we feel; that we shall never forgive him, that we can't endure it."

"He'll think I'm cheeky," her brother returned, looking down at his papers with his back to her and his hands in his pockets.

"Cheeky to plead for *her* memory?"

"He'll say it's none of my business."

"Then you believe he'll do it?" cried the girl.

"Not a bit. Go to bed!"

19

"*I'll* speak to him"—she had turned as pale as a young priestess.

"Don't cry out till you're hurt; wait till he speaks to *you*."

"He won't, he won't!" she declared. "He'll do it without telling us."

Her brother had faced round to her again; he started a little at this, and again, at one of the candles, lighted his cigarette, which had gone out. She looked at him a moment; then he said something that surprised her. "Is Mrs. Churchley very rich?"

"I haven't the least idea. What on earth has that to do with it?"

Godfrey puffed his cigarette. "Does she live as if she were?"

"She has a lot of hideous showy things."

"Well, we must keep our eyes open," he concluded. "And now you *must* let me get on." He kissed his visitor as if to make up for dismissing her, or for his failure to take fire; and she held him a moment, burying her head on his shoulder.

A wave of emotion surged through her, and again she quavered out: "Ah why did she leave us? Why did she leave us?"

"Yes, why indeed?" the young man sighed, disengaging himself with a movement of oppression.

ADELA was so far right as that by the end of the week, though she remained certain, her father had still not made the announcement she dreaded. What convinced her was the sense of her changed relations with him—of there being between them something unexpressed, something she was aware of as she would have been of an open wound. When she spoke of this to Godfrey he said the change was of her own making—also that she was cruelly unjust to the governor. She suffered even more from her brother's unexpected perversity; she had had so different a theory about him that her disappointment was almost an humiliation and she needed all her fortitude to pitch her faith lower. She wondered what had happened to him and why he so failed her. She would have trusted him to feel right about anything, above all about such a question. Their worship of their mother's memory, their recognition of her sacred place in their past, her exquisite influence in their father's life, his fortune, his career, in the whole history of the family and welfare of the house—accomplished clever gentle good beautiful and capable as she had been, a woman whose quiet distinction was universally admired, so that on her death one of the Princesses, the most august of her friends, had written Adela such a note about her as princesses were understood very seldom to write: their hushed tenderness over all this was like a religion, and was also an attributive honour, to fall away from which was a form of treachery. This wasn't the way people usually felt in London, she knew; but strenuous ardent observant girl as she was, with secrecies of sentiment and dim originalities of attitude, she had already made up her mind that London was no treasure-house of delicacies. Remembrance there was hammered thin—to be faithful was to make society gape. The patient dead were sacrificed; they had no shrines, for people were literally ashamed of mourning. When they had hustled all sensibility out of their lives they invented the fiction that they felt too much to utter. Adela said nothing to her sisters; this reticence was part of the virtue it was her idea to practise for them. *She* was to be their mother, a direct deputy and representative. Before the vision of that other woman parading in such a character she felt capable of ingenuities, of deep diplomacies. The essence of these indeed was just tremulously to watch her father. Five days after they had dined together at Mrs. Churchley's he asked her if she had been to see that lady.

"No indeed, why should I?" Adela knew that he knew she hadn't been, since Mrs. Churchley would have told him.

"Don't you call on people after you dine with them?" said Colonel Chart.

"Yes, in the course of time. I don't rush off within the week."

Her father looked at her, and his eyes were colder than she had ever seen them, which was probably, she reflected, just the way hers appeared to himself. "Then you'll please rush off to-morrow. She's to dine with us on the 12th, and I shall expect your sisters to come down."

Adela stared. "To a dinner-party?"

"It's not to be a dinner-party. I want them to know Mrs. Churchley."

"Is there to be nobody else?"

"Godfrey of course. A family party," he said with an assurance before which she turned cold.

The girl asked her brother that evening if *that* wasn't tantamount to an announcement. He looked at her queerly and then said: "*I've* been to see her."

"What on earth did you do that for?"

"Father told me he wished it."

"Then he *has* told you?"

"Told me what?" Godfrey asked while her heart sank with the sense of his making difficulties for her.

"That they're engaged, of course. What else can all this mean?"

"He didn't tell me that, but I like her."

"*Like* her!" the girl shrieked.

"She's very kind, very good."

"To thrust herself upon us when we hate her? Is that what you call kind? Is that what you call decent?"

"Oh *I* don't hate her"—and he turned away as if she bored him.

She called the next day on Mrs. Churchley, designing to break out somehow, to plead, to appeal—"Oh spare us! have mercy on us! let him alone! go away!" But that wasn't easy when they were face to face. Mrs. Churchley had every intention of getting, as she would have said—she was perpetually using the expression—into touch; but her good intentions were as depressing as a tailor's misfits. She could never understand that they had no place for her vulgar charity, that their life was filled with a fragrance of perfection for which she had no sense fine enough. She was as undomestic as a shop-front and as out of tune as a parrot. She would either make them live in the streets or bring the streets into their life—it was the same thing. She had evidently never read a book, and she used intonations that Adela had never heard, as if she had been an Australian or an American. She understood everything in a vulgar sense; speaking of Godfrey's visit to her and praising him according to her idea, saying horrid things about him—that he was awfully good-looking, a perfect gentleman, the kind she liked. How could her father, who was after all in everything else such a dear, listen to a woman, or endure her, who thought she pleased him when she called the son of his dead wife a perfect gentleman? What would he have been, pray? Much she knew about what any of them were! When she told Adela she wanted her to like her the girl thought for an instant her opportunity had come—the chance to plead with her and beg her off. But she presented such an impenetrable surface that it would have been like giving a message to a varnished door. She wasn't a woman, said Adela; she was an address.

When she dined in Seymour Street the "children," as the girl called the others, including Godfrey, liked her. Beatrice and Muriel stared shyly and silently at the wonders of her apparel (she was brutally over-dressed) without of course guessing the danger that tainted the air. They supposed her in their innocence to be amusing, and they didn't know, any more than she did herself, how she patronised them. When she was upstairs with them after dinner Adela could see her look round the room at the things she meant to alter—their mother's things, not a bit like her own and not good enough for her. After a quarter of an hour of this our young lady felt sure she was deciding that Seymour Street wouldn't do at all, the dear old home that had done for their mother those twenty years. Was she plotting to transport them all to her horrible Prince's Gate? Of one thing at any rate Adela was certain: her father, at that moment alone in the dining-room with Godfrey, pretending to drink another glass of wine to make time, was coming to the point, was telling the news. When they reappeared they both, to her eyes, looked unnatural: the news had been told.

She had it from Godfrey before Mrs. Churchley left the house, when, after a brief interval, he followed her out of the drawing-room on her taking her sisters to bed. She was waiting for him at the door of her room. Her father was then alone with his *fiancée*—the word was grotesque to Adela; it was already as if the place were her home.

"What did you say to him?" our young woman asked when her brother had told her.

"I said nothing." Then he added, colouring—the expression of her face was such—"There was nothing to say."

"Is that how it strikes you?"—and she stared at the lamp.

"He asked me to speak to her," Godfrey went on.

"In what hideous sense?"

"To tell her I was glad."

"And did you?" Adela panted.

"I don't know. I said something. She kissed me."

"Oh how *could* you?" shuddered the girl, who covered her face with her hands.

24

"He says she's very rich," her brother returned.

"Is that why you kissed her?"

"I didn't kiss her. Good-night." And the young man, turning his back, went out.

When he had gone Adela locked herself in as with the fear she should be overtaken or invaded, and during a sleepless feverish memorable night she took counsel of her uncompromising spirit. She saw things as they were, in all the indignity of life. The levity, the mockery, the infidelity, the ugliness, lay as plain as a map before her; it was a world of gross practical jokes, a world *pour rire*; but she cried about it all the same. The morning dawned early, or rather it seemed to her there had been no night, nothing but a sickly creeping day. But by the time she heard the house stirring again she had determined what to do. When she came down to the breakfast-room her father was already in his place with newspapers and letters; and she expected the first words he would utter to be a rebuke to her for having disappeared the night before without taking leave of Mrs. Churchley. Then she saw he wished to be intensely kind, to make every allowance, to conciliate and console her. He knew she had heard from Godfrey, and he got up and kissed her. He told her as quickly as possible, to have it over, stammering a little, with an "I've a piece of news for you that will probably shock you," yet looking even exaggeratedly grave and rather pompous, to inspire the respect he didn't deserve. When he kissed her she melted, she burst into tears. He held her against him, kissing her again and again, saying tenderly "Yes, yes, I know, I know." But he didn't know else he couldn't have done it. Beatrice and Muriel came in, frightened when they saw her crying, and still more scared when she turned to them with words and an air that were terrible in their comfortable little lives: "Papa's going to be married; he's going to marry Mrs. Churchley!" After staring a moment and seeing their father look as strange, on his side, as Adela, though in a different way, the children also began to cry, so that when the servants arrived with tea and boiled eggs these functionaries were greatly embarrassed with their burden, not knowing whether to come in or hang back. They all scraped together a decorum, and as soon as the things had been put on table the Colonel banished the men with a glance. Then he made a little affectionate speech to Beatrice and Muriel, in which he described Mrs. Churchley as the kindest, the most delightful of women, only wanting to make them happy, only wanting to make *him* happy, and convinced that he would be if they were and that they would be if he was.

"What do such words mean?" Adela asked herself. She declared privately that they meant nothing, but she was silent, and every one was silent, on account of the advent of Miss Flynn the governess, before whom Colonel Chart preferred not to discuss the situation. Adela recognised on the spot that if things were to go as he wished his children would practically never again be alone with him. He would spend all his time with Mrs. Churchley till they were married, and then Mrs. Churchley would spend all her time with him. Adela was ashamed of him, and that was horrible—all the more that every one else would be, all his other friends, every one who had known her mother. But the public dishonour to that high memory shouldn't be enacted; he shouldn't do as he wished.

After breakfast her father remarked to her that it would give him pleasure if in a day or two she would take her sisters to see their friend, and she replied that he should be obeyed. He held her hand a moment, looking at her with an argument in his eyes which presently hardened into sternness. He wanted to know that she forgave him, but also wanted to assure her that he expected her to mind what she did, to go straight. She turned away her eyes; she was indeed ashamed of him.

She waited three days and then conveyed her sisters to the *repaire*, as she would have been ready to term it, of the lioness. That queen of beasts was surrounded with callers, as Adela knew she would be; it was her "day" and the occasion the girl preferred. Before this she had spent all her time with her companions, talking to them about their mother, playing on their memory of her, making them cry and making them laugh, reminding them of blest hours of their early childhood, telling them anecdotes of her own. None the less she confided to them that she believed there was no harm at all in Mrs. Churchley, and that when the time should come she would probably take them out immensely. She saw with smothered irritation that they enjoyed their visit at Prince's Gate; they had never been at anything so "grown-up," nor seen so many smart bonnets and brilliant complexions. Moreover they were considered with interest, quite as if, being minor elements, yet perceptible ones, of Mrs. Churchley's new life, they had been described in advance and were the heroines of the occasion. There were so many ladies present that this personage didn't talk to them much; she only called them her "chicks" and asked them to hand about tea-cups and bread and butter. All of which was highly agreeable and indeed intensely exciting to Beatrice and Muriel, who had little round red spots in *their* cheeks when they came away. Adela quivered with the sense that her mother's children were now Mrs. Churchley's "chicks" and a part of the furniture of Mrs. Churchley's dreadful consciousness.

It was one thing to have made up her mind, however; it was another thing to make her attempt. It was when she learned from Godfrey that the day was fixed, the 20th of July, only six weeks removed, that she felt the importance of prompt action. She learned everything from Godfrey now, having decided it would be hypocrisy to question her father. Even her silence was hypocritical, but she couldn't weep and wail. Her father showed extreme tact; taking no notice of her detachment, treating it as a moment of *bouderie* he was bound to allow her and that would pout itself away. She debated much as to whether she should take Godfrey into her confidence; she would have done so without hesitation if he hadn't disappointed her. He was so little what she might have expected, and so perversely preoccupied that she could explain it only by the high pressure at which he was living, his anxiety about his "exam." He was in a fidget, in a fever, putting on a spurt to come in first; sceptical moreover about his success and cynical about everything else. He appeared to agree to the general axiom that they didn't want a strange woman thrust into their life, but he found Mrs. Churchley "very jolly as a person to know." He had been to see her by himself—he had been to see her three times. He in fact gave it out that he would make the most of her now; he should probably be so little in Seymour Street after these days. What Adela at last determined to give him was her assurance that the marriage would never take place. When he asked what she meant and who was to prevent it she replied that the interesting couple would abandon the idea of themselves, or that Mrs. Churchley at least would after a week or two back out of it.

"That will be really horrid then," Godfrey pronounced. "The only respectable thing, at the point they've come to, is to put it through. Charming for poor Dad to have the air of being 'chucked'!"

This made her hesitate two days more, but she found answers more valid than any objections. The many-voiced answer to everything—it was like the autumn wind round the house—was the affront that fell back on her mother. Her mother was dead but it killed her again. So one morning at eleven o'clock, when she knew her father was writing letters, she went out quietly and, stopping the first hansom she met, drove to Prince's Gate. Mrs. Churchley was at home, and she was shown into the drawing-room with the request that she would wait five minutes. She waited without the sense of breaking down at the last, and the impulse to run away, which were what she had expected to have. In the cab and at the door her heart had beat terribly, but now suddenly, with the game really to play, she found herself lucid and calm. It was a joy to her to feel later that this was the way Mrs. Churchley found her: not confused, not stammering nor prevaricating, only a little amazed at her own courage, conscious of the immense responsibility of her step and wonderfully older than her years. Her hostess sounded her at first with suspicious eyes, but eventually, to Adela's surprise, burst into tears. At this the girl herself cried, and with the secret happiness of believing they were saved. Mrs. Churchley said she would think over what she had been told, and she promised her young friend, freely enough and very firmly, not to betray the secret of the latter's step to the Colonel. They were saved—they were saved: the words sung themselves in the girl's soul as she came downstairs. When the door opened for her she saw her brother on the step, and they looked at each other in surprise, each finding it on the part of the other an odd hour for Prince's Gate. Godfrey remarked that Mrs. Churchley would have enough of the family, and Adela answered that she would perhaps have too much. None the less the young man went in while his sister took her way home.

III

SHE saw nothing of him for nearly a week; he had more and more his own times and hours, adjusted to his tremendous responsibilities, and he spent whole days at his crammer's. When she knocked at his door late in the evening he was regularly not in his room. It was known in the house how much he was worried; he was horribly nervous about his ordeal. It was to begin on the 23rd of June, and his father was as worried as himself. The wedding had been arranged in relation to this; they wished poor Godfrey's fate settled first, though they felt the nuptials would be darkened if it shouldn't be settled right.

Ten days after that performance of her private undertaking Adela began to sniff, as it were, a difference in the general air; but as yet she was afraid to exult. It wasn't in truth a difference for the better, so that there might be still a great tension. Her father, since the announcement of his intended marriage, had been visibly pleased with himself, but that pleasure now appeared to have undergone a check. She had the impression known to the passengers on a great steamer when, in the middle of the night, they feel the engines stop. As this impression may easily sharpen to the sense that something serious has happened, so the girl asked herself what had actually occurred. She had expected something serious; but it was as if she couldn't keep still in her cabin—she wanted to go up and see. On the 20th, just before breakfast, her maid brought her a message from her brother. Mr. Godfrey would be obliged if she would speak to him in his room. She went straight up to him, dreading to find him ill, broken down on the eve of his formidable week. This was not the case however—he rather seemed already at work, to have been at work since dawn. But he was very white and his eyes had a strange and new expression. Her beautiful young brother looked older; he looked haggard and hard. He met her there as if he had been waiting for her, and he said at once: "Please tell me this, Adela—what was the purpose of your visit the other morning to Mrs. Churchley, the day I met you at her door?"

She stared—she cast about. "The purpose? What's the matter? Why do you ask?"

"They've put it off—they've put it off a month."

"Ah thank God!" said Adela.

"Why the devil do you thank God?" Godfrey asked with a strange impatience.

She gave a strained intense smile. "You know I think it all wrong."

He stood looking at her up and down. "What did you do there? How did you interfere?"

"Who told you I interfered?" she returned with a deep flush.

"You said something—you did something. I knew you had done it when I saw you come out."

"What I did was my own business."

"Damn your own business!" cried the young man.

She had never in her life been so spoken to, and in advance, had she been given the choice, would have said that she'd rather die than be so handled by Godfrey. But her spirit was high, and for a moment she was as angry as if she had been cut with a whip. She escaped the blow but felt the insult. "And *your* business then?" she asked. "I wondered what that was when I saw *you*."

He stood a moment longer scowling at her; then with the exclamation "You've made a pretty mess!" he turned away from her and sat down to his books.

They had put it off, as he said; her father was dry and stiff and official about it. "I suppose I had better let you know we've thought it best to postpone our marriage till the end of the summer—Mrs. Churchley has so many arrangements to make": he was not more expansive than that. She neither knew nor greatly cared whether she but vainly imagined or correctly observed him to watch her obliquely for some measure of her receipt of these words. She flattered herself that, thanks to Godfrey's forewarning, cruel as the form of it had been, she was able to repress any crude sign of elation. She had a perfectly good conscience, for she could now judge what odious elements Mrs. Churchley, whom she had not seen since the morning in Prince's Gate, had already introduced into their dealings. She gathered without difficulty that her father hadn't concurred in the postponement, for he was more restless than before, more absent and distinctly irritable. There was naturally still the question of how much of this condition was to be attributed to his solicitude about Godfrey. That young man took occasion to say a horrible thing to his sister: "If I don't pass it will be your fault." These were dreadful days for the girl, and she asked herself how she could have borne them if the hovering spirit of her mother hadn't been at her side. Fortunately she always felt it there, sustaining, commending, sanctifying. Suddenly her father announced to her that he wished her to go immediately, with her sisters, down to Brinton, where there was always part of a household and where for a few weeks they would manage well enough. The only explanation he gave of this desire was that he wanted them out of the way. "Out of the way of what?" she queried, since there were to be for the time no preparations in Seymour Street. She was willing to take it for out of the way of his nerves.

She never needed urging however to go to Brinton, the dearest old house in the world, where the happiest days of her young life had been spent and the silent nearness of her mother always seemed greatest. She was happy again, with Beatrice and Muriel and Miss Flynn, with the air of summer and the haunted rooms and her mother's garden and the talking oaks and the nightingales. She wrote briefly to her father, giving him, as he had requested, an account of things; and he wrote back that since she was so contented—she didn't recognise having told him that—she had better not return to town at all. The fag-end of the London season would be unimportant to her, and he was getting on very well. He mentioned that Godfrey had passed his tests, but, as she knew, there would be a tiresome wait before news of results. The poor chap was going abroad for a month with young Sherard—he had earned a little rest and a little fun. He went abroad without a word to Adela, but in his beautiful little hand he took a chaffing leave of Beatrice. The child showed her sister the letter, of which she was very proud and which contained no message for any one else. This was the worst bitterness of the whole crisis for that somebody—its placing in so strange a light the creature in the world whom, after her mother, she had loved best.

Colonel Chart had said he would "run down" while his children were at Brinton, but they heard no more about it. He only wrote two or three times to Miss Flynn on matters in regard to which Adela was surprised he shouldn't have communicated with herself. Muriel accomplished an upright little letter to Mrs. Churchley—her eldest sister neither fostered nor discouraged the performance—to which Mrs. Churchley replied, after a fortnight, in a meagre and, as Adela thought, illiterate fashion, making no allusion to the approach of any closer tie. Evidently the situation had changed; the question of the marriage was dropped, at any rate for the time. This idea gave our young woman a singular and almost intoxicating sense of power; she felt as if she were riding a great wave of confidence. She had decided and acted—the greatest could do no more than that. The grand thing was to see one's results, and what else was she doing? These results were in big rich conspicuous lives; the stage was large on which she moved her figures. Such a vision was exciting, and as they had the use of a couple of ponies at Brinton she worked off her excitement by a long gallop. A day or two after this however came news of which the effect was to rekindle it. Godfrey had come back, the list had been published, he had passed first. These happy tidings proceeded from the young man himself; he announced them by a telegram to Beatrice, who had never in her life before received such a missive and was proportionately inflated. Adela reflected that she herself ought to have felt snubbed, but she was too happy. They were free again, they were themselves, the nightmare of the previous weeks was blown away, the unity and dignity of her father's life restored, and, to round off her sense of success, Godfrey had achieved his first step toward high distinction. She wrote him the next day as frankly and affectionately as if there had been no estrangement between them, and besides telling him how she rejoiced in his triumph begged him in charity to let them know exactly how the case stood with regard to Mrs. Churchley.

Late in the summer afternoon she walked through the park to the village with her letter, posted it and came back. Suddenly, at one of the turns of the avenue, half-way to the house, she saw a young man hover there as if awaiting her—a young man who proved to be Godfrey on his pedestrian progress over from the station. He had seen her as he took his short cut, and if he had come down to Brinton it wasn't apparently to avoid her. There was nevertheless none of the joy of his triumph in his face as he came a very few steps to meet her; and although, stiffly enough, he let her kiss him and say "I'm so glad—I'm so glad!" she felt this tolerance as not quite the mere calm of the rising diplomatist. He turned toward the house with her and walked on a short distance while she uttered the hope that he had come to stay some days.

"Only till to-morrow morning. They're sending me straight to Madrid. I came down to say good-bye; there's a fellow bringing my bags."

"To Madrid? How awfully nice! And it's awfully nice of you to have come," she said as she passed her hand into his arm.

The movement made him stop, and, stopping, he turned on her in a flash a face of something more than, suspicion—of passionate reprobation. "What I really came for—you might as well know without more delay—is to ask you a question."

"A question?"—she echoed it with a beating heart.

They stood there under the old trees in the lingering light, and, young and fine and fair as they both were, formed a complete superficial harmony with the peaceful English scene. A near view, however, would have shown that Godfrey Chart hadn't taken so much trouble only to skim the surface. He looked deep into his sister's eyes. "What was it you said that morning to Mrs. Churchley?"

She fixed them on the ground a moment, but at last met his own again. "If she has told you, why do you ask?"

"She has told me nothing. I've seen for myself."

"What have you seen?"

"She has broken it off. Everything's over. Father's in the depths."

33

"In the depths?" the girl quavered.

"Did you think it would make him jolly?" he went on.

She had to choose what to say. "He'll get over it. He'll be glad."

"That remains to be seen. You interfered, you invented something, you got round her. I insist on knowing what you did."

Adela felt that if it was a question of obstinacy there was something within her she could count on; in spite of which, while she stood looking down again a moment, she said to herself "I could be dumb and dogged if I chose, but I scorn to be." She wasn't ashamed of what she had done, but she wanted to be clear. "Are you absolutely certain it's broken off?"

"He is, and she is; so that's as good."

"What reason has she given?"

"None at all—or half a dozen; it's the same thing. She has changed her mind—she mistook her feelings—she can't part with her independence. Moreover he has too many children."

"Did he tell you this?" the girl asked.

"Mrs. Churchley told me. She has gone abroad for a year."

"And she didn't tell you what I said to her?"

Godfrey showed an impatience. "Why should I take this trouble if she had?"

"You might have taken it to make me suffer," said Adela. "That appears to be what you want to do."

"No, I leave that to you—it's the good turn you've done me!" cried the young man with hot tears in his eyes.

She stared, aghast with the perception that there was some dreadful thing she didn't know; but he walked on, dropping the question angrily and turning his back to her as if he couldn't trust himself. She read his disgust in his averted, face, in the way he squared his shoulders and smote the ground with his stick, and she hurried after him and presently overtook him. She kept by him for a moment in silence; then she broke out: "What do you mean? What in the world have I done to you?"

"She would have helped me. She was all ready to help me," Godfrey portentously said.

"Helped you in what?" She wondered what he meant; if he had made debts that he was afraid to confess to his father and—of all horrible things—had been looking to Mrs. Churchley to pay. She turned red with the mere apprehension of this and, on the heels of her guess, exulted again at having perhaps averted such a shame.

"Can't you just see I'm in trouble? Where are your eyes, your senses, your sympathy, that you talk so much about? Haven't you seen these six months that I've a curst worry in my life?"

She seized his arm, made him stop, stood looking up at him like a frightened little girl. "What's the matter, Godfrey?—what *is* the matter?"

"You've gone against me so—I could strangle you!" he growled. This image added nothing to her dread; her dread was that he had done some wrong, was stained with some guilt. She uttered it to him with clasped hands, begging him to tell her the worst; but, still more passionately, he cut her short with his own cry: "In God's name, satisfy me! What infernal thing did you do?"

"It wasn't infernal—it was right. I told her mamma had been wretched," said Adela.

"Wretched? You told her such a lie?"

"It was the only way, and she believed me."

"Wretched how?—wretched when?—wretched where?" the young man stammered.

"I told her papa had made her so, and that *she* ought to know it. I told her the question troubled me unspeakably, but that I had made up my mind

35

it was my duty to initiate her." Adela paused, the light of bravado in her face, as if, though struck while the words came with the monstrosity of what she had done, she was incapable of abating a jot of it. "I notified her that he had faults and peculiarities that made mamma's life a long worry—a martyrdom that she hid wonderfully from the world, but that we saw and that I had often pitied. I told her what they were, these faults and peculiarities; I put the dots on the i's. I said it wasn't fair to let another person marry him without a warning. I warned her; I satisfied my conscience. She could do as she liked. My responsibility was over."

Godfrey gazed at her; he listened with parted lips, incredulous and appalled. "You invented such a tissue of falsities and calumnies, and you talk about your conscience? You stand there in your senses and proclaim your crime?"

"I'd have committed any crime that would have rescued us."

"You insult and blacken and ruin your own father?" Godfrey kept on.

"He'll never know it; she took a vow she wouldn't tell him."

"Ah I'll be damned if *I* won't tell him!" he rang out.

Adela felt sick at this, but she flamed up to resent the treachery, as it struck her, of such a menace. "I did right—I did right!" she vehemently declared "I went down on my knees to pray for guidance, and I saved mamma's memory from outrage. But if I hadn't, if I hadn't"—she faltered an instant—"I'm not worse than you, and I'm not so bad, for you've done something that you're ashamed to tell me."

He had taken out his watch; he looked at it with quick intensity, as if not hearing nor heeding her. Then, his calculating eyes raised, he fixed her long enough to exclaim with unsurpassable horror and contempt: "You raving maniac!" He turned away from her; he bounded down the avenue in the direction from which they had come, and, while she watched him, strode away, across the grass, toward the short cut to the station.

IV

His bags, by the time she got home, had been brought to the house, but Beatrice and Muriel, immediately informed of this, waited for their brother in vain. Their sister said nothing to them of her having seen him, and she accepted after a little, with a calmness that surprised herself, the idea that he had returned to town to denounce her. She believed this would make no difference now—she had done what she had done. She had somehow a stiff faith in Mrs. Churchley. Once that so considerable mass had received its impetus it wouldn't, it couldn't pull up. It represented a heavy-footed person, incapable of further agility. Adela recognised too how well it might have come over her that there were too many children. Lastly the girl fortified herself with the reflexion, grotesque in the conditions and conducing to prove her sense of humour not high, that her father was after all not a man to be played with. It seemed to her at any rate that if she *had* baffled his unholy purpose she could bear anything—bear imprisonment and bread and water, bear lashes and torture, bear even his lifelong reproach. What she could bear least was the wonder of the inconvenience she had inflicted on Godfrey. She had time to turn this over, very vainly, for a succession of days—days more numerous than she had expected, which passed without bringing her from London any summons to come up and take her punishment. She sounded the possible, she compared the degrees of the probable; feeling however that as a cloistered girl she was poorly equipped for speculation. She tried to imagine the calamitous things young men might do, and could only feel that such things would naturally be connected either with borrowed money or with bad women. She became conscious that after all she knew almost nothing about either of those interests. The worst woman she knew was Mrs. Churchley herself. Meanwhile there was no reverberation from Seymour Street—only a sultry silence.

At Brinton she spent hours in her mother's garden, where she had grown up, where she considered that she was training for old age, since she meant not to depend on whist. She loved the place as, had she been a good Catholic, she would have loved the smell of her parish church; and indeed there was in her passion for flowers something of the respect of a religion. They seemed to her the only things in the world that really respected themselves, unless one made an exception for Nutkins, who had been in command all through her mother's time, with whom she had had a real friendship and who had been affected by their pure example. He was the person left in the world with whom on the whole she could speak most intimately of the dead. They never had to name her together—they only said "she"; and Nutkins freely conceded that she had taught him everything he knew. When Beatrice and Muriel said "she" they referred to Mrs. Churchley. Adela had reason to believe she should never marry, and that some day she should have about a thousand a year. This made her see in the far future a little garden of her own, under a hill, full of rare and exquisite things, where she would spend most of her old age on her knees with an apron and stout gloves, with a pair of shears and a trowel, steeped in the comfort of being thought mad.

One morning ten days after her scene with Godfrey, on coming back into the house shortly before lunch, she was met by Miss Flynn with the notification that a lady in the drawing-room had been waiting for her for some minutes. "A lady" suggested immediately Mrs. Churchley. It came over Adela that the form in which her penalty was to descend would be a personal explanation with that misdirected woman. The lady had given no name, and Miss Flynn hadn't seen Mrs. Churchley; nevertheless the governess was certain Adela's surmise was wrong.

"Is she big and dreadful?" the girl asked.

Miss Flynn, who was circumspection itself, took her time. "She's dreadful, but she's not big." She added that she wasn't sure she ought to let Adela go in alone; but this young lady took herself throughout for a heroine, and it wasn't in a heroine to shrink from any encounter. Wasn't she every instant in transcendent contact with her mother? The visitor might have no connexion whatever with the drama of her father's frustrated marriage; but everything to-day for Adela was part of that.

Miss Flynn's description had prepared her for a considerable shock, but she wasn't agitated by her first glimpse of the person who awaited her. A youngish well-dressed woman stood there, and silence was between them while they looked at each other. Before either had spoken however Adela began to see what Miss Flynn had intended. In the light of the drawing-room window the lady was five-and-thirty years of age and had vivid yellow hair. She also had a blue cloth suit with brass buttons, a stick-up collar like a gentleman's, a necktie arranged in a sailor's knot, a golden pin in the shape of a little lawn-tennis racket, and pearl-grey gloves with big black stitchings. Adela's second impression was that she was an actress, and her third that no such person had ever before crossed that threshold.

"I'll tell you what I've come for," said the apparition. "I've come to ask you to intercede." She wasn't an actress; an actress would have had a nicer voice.

"To intercede?" Adela was too bewildered to ask her to sit down.

"With your father, you know. He doesn't know, but he'll have to." Her "have" sounded like "'ave." She explained, with many more such sounds, that she was Mrs. Godfrey, that they had been married seven mortal months. If Godfrey was going abroad she must go with him, and the only way she could go with him would be for his father to do something. He was afraid of his father—that was clear; he was afraid even to tell him. What she had come down for was to see some other member of the family face to face—"fice to fice," Mrs. Godfrey called it—and try if he couldn't be approached by another side. If no one else would act then she would just have to act herself. The Colonel would have to do something—that was the only way out of it.

What really happened Adela never quite understood; what seemed to be happening was that the room went round and round. Through the blur of perception accompanying this effect the sharp stabs of her visitor's revelation came to her like the words heard by a patient "going off" under ether. She afterwards denied passionately even to herself that she had done anything so abject as to faint; but there was a lapse in her consciousness on the score of Miss Flynn's intervention. This intervention had evidently been active, for when they talked the matter over, later in the day, with bated breath and infinite dissimulation for the school-room quarter, the governess had more lurid truths, and still more, to impart than to receive. She was at any rate under the impression that she had athletically contended, in the drawing-room, with the yellow hair—this after removing Adela from the scene and before inducing Mrs. Godfrey to withdraw. Miss Flynn had never known a more thrilling day, for all the rest of it too was pervaded with agitations and conversations, precautions and alarms. It was given out to Beatrice and Muriel that their sister had been taken suddenly ill, and the governess ministered to her in her room. Indeed Adela had never found herself less at ease, for this time she had received a blow that she couldn't return. There was nothing to do but to take it, to endure the humiliation of her wound.

At first she declined to take it—having, as might appear, the much more attractive resource of regarding her visitant as a mere masquerading person, an impudent impostor. On the face of the matter moreover it wasn't fair to believe till one heard; and to hear in such a case was to hear Godfrey himself. Whatever she had tried to imagine about him she hadn't arrived at anything so belittling as an idiotic secret marriage with a dyed and painted hag. Adela repeated this last word as if it gave her comfort; and indeed where everything was so bad fifteen years of seniority made the case little worse. Miss Flynn was portentous, for Miss Flynn had had it out with the wretch. She had cross-questioned her and had not broken her down. This was the most uplifted hour of Miss Flynn's life; for whereas she usually had to content herself with being humbly and gloomily in the right she could now be magnanimously and showily so. Her only perplexity was as to what she ought to do—write to Colonel Chart or go up to town to see him. She bloomed with alternatives—she resembled some dull garden-path which under a copious downpour has begun to flaunt with colour. Toward evening Adela was obliged to recognise that her brother's worry, of which he had spoken to her, had appeared bad enough to consist even of a low wife, and to remember that, so far from its being inconceivable a young man in his position should clandestinely take one, she had been present, years before, during her mother's lifetime, when Lady Molesley declared gaily, over a cup of tea, that this was precisely what she expected of her eldest son. The next morning it was the worst possibilities that seemed clearest; the only thing left with a tatter of dusky comfort being the ambiguity of Godfrey's charge that her own action had "done" for him.

That was a matter by itself, and she racked her brains for a connecting link between Mrs. Churchley and Mrs. Godfrey. At last she made up her mind that they were related by blood; very likely, though differing in fortune, they were cousins or even sisters. But even then what did the wretched boy mean?

Arrested by the unnatural fascination of opportunity, Miss Flynn received before lunch a telegram from Colonel Chart—an order for dinner and a vehicle; he and Godfrey were to arrive at six o'clock. Adela had plenty of occupation for the interval, since she was pitying her father when she wasn't rejoicing that her mother had gone too soon to know. She flattered herself she made out the providential reason of that cruelty now. She found time however still to wonder for what purpose, given the situation, Godfrey was to be brought down. She wasn't unconscious indeed that she had little general knowledge of what usually was done with young men in that predicament. One talked about the situation, but the situation was an abyss. She felt this still more when she found, on her father's arrival, that nothing apparently was to happen as she had taken for granted it would. There was an inviolable hush over the whole affair, but no tragedy, no publicity, nothing ugly. The tragedy had been in town—the faces of the two men spoke of it in spite of their other perfunctory aspects; and at present there was only a family dinner, with Beatrice and Muriel and the governess—with almost a company tone too, the result of the desire to avoid publicity. Adela admired her father; she knew what he was feeling if Mrs. Godfrey had been at him, and yet she saw him positively gallant. He was mildly austere, or rather even—what was it?—august; just as, coldly equivocal, he never looked at his son, so that at moments he struck her as almost sick with sadness. Godfrey was equally inscrutable and therefore wholly different from what he had been as he stood before her in the park. If he was to start on his career (with such a wife!— wouldn't she utterly blight it?) he was already professional enough to know how to wear a mask.

Before they rose from table she felt herself wholly bewildered, so little were such large causes traceable in their effects. She had nerved herself for a great ordeal, but the air was as sweet as an anodyne. It was perfectly plain to her that her father was deadly sore—as pathetic as a person betrayed. He was broken, but he showed no resentment; there was a weight on his heart, but he had lightened it by dressing as immaculately as usual for dinner. She asked herself what immensity of a row there could have been in town to have left his anger so spent. He went through everything, even to sitting with his son after dinner. When they came out together he invited Beatrice and Muriel to the billiard-room, and as Miss Flynn discreetly withdrew Adela was left alone with Godfrey, who was completely changed and not now in the least of a rage. He was broken too, but not so pathetic as his father. He was only very correct and apologetic he said to his sister: "I'm awfully sorry *you* were annoyed—it was something I never dreamed of."

She couldn't think immediately what he meant; then she grasped the reference to her extraordinary invader. She was uncertain, however, what tone to take; perhaps his father had arranged with him that they were to make the best of it. But she spoke her own despair in the way she murmured "Oh Godfrey, Godfrey, is it true?"

"I've been the most unutterable donkey—you can say what you like to me. You can't say anything worse than I've said to myself."

"My brother, my brother!"—his words made her wail it out. He hushed her with a movement and she asked: "What has father said?"

He looked very high over her head. "He'll give her six hundred a year."

"Ah the angel!"—it was too splendid.

"On condition"—Godfrey scarce blinked—"she never comes near me. She has solemnly promised, and she'll probably leave me alone to get the money. If she doesn't—in diplomacy—I'm lost." He had been turning his eyes vaguely about, this way and that, to avoid meeting hers; but after another instant he gave up the effort and she had the miserable confession of his glance. "I've been living in hell."

"My brother, my brother!" she yearningly repeated.

"I'm not an idiot; yet for her I've behaved like one. Don't ask me—you mustn't know. It was all done in a day, and since then fancy my condition; fancy my work in such a torment; fancy my coming through at all."

"Thank God you passed!" she cried. "You were wonderful!"

"I'd have shot myself if I hadn't been. I had an awful day yesterday with the governor; it was late at night before it was over. I leave England next week. He brought me down here for it to look well—so that the children shan't know."

"*He's* wonderful too!" Adela murmured.

"Wonderful too!" Godfrey echoed.

"Did *she* tell him?" the girl went on.

"She came straight to Seymour Street from here. She saw him alone first; then he called me in. *That* luxury lasted about an hour."

"Poor, poor father!" Adela moaned at this; on which her brother remained silent. Then after he had alluded to it as the scene he had lived in terror of all through his cramming, and she had sighed forth again her pity and admiration for such a mixture of anxieties and such a triumph of talent, she pursued: "Have you told him?"

"Told him what?"

"What you said you would—what *I* did."

Godfrey turned away as if at present he had very little interest in that inferior tribulation. "I was angry with you, but I cooled off. I held my tongue."

She clasped her hands. "You thought of mamma!"

"Oh don't speak of mamma!" he cried as in rueful tenderness.

It was indeed not a happy moment, and she murmured: "No; if you *had* thought of her—!"

This made Godfrey face her again with a small flare in his eyes. "Oh *then* it didn't prevent. I thought that woman really good. I believed in her."

"Is she *very* bad?"

"I shall never mention her to you again," he returned with dignity.

"You may believe *I* won't speak of her! So father doesn't know?" the girl added.

"Doesn't know what?"

"That I said what I did to Mrs. Churchley."

He had a momentary pause. "I don't think so, but you must find out for yourself."

"I shall find out," said Adela. "But what had Mrs. Churchley to do with it?"

"With *my* misery? I told her. I had to tell some one."

"Why didn't you tell me?"

He appeared—though but after an instant—to know exactly why. "Oh you take things so beastly hard—you make such rows." Adela covered her face with her hands and he went on: "What I wanted was comfort—not to be lashed up. I thought I should go mad. I wanted Mrs. Churchley to break it to father, to intercede for me and help him to meet it. She was awfully kind to me, she listened and she understood; she could fancy how it had happened. Without her I shouldn't have pulled through. She liked me, you know," he further explained, and as if it were quite worth mentioning—all the more that it was pleasant to him. "She said she'd do what she could for me. She was full of sympathy and resource. I really leaned on her. But when *you* cut in of course it spoiled everything. That's why I was so furious with you. She couldn't do anything then."

Adela dropped her hands, staring; she felt she had walked in darkness. "So that he had to meet it alone?"

"*Dame!*" said Godfrey, who had got up his French tremendously.

Muriel came to the door to say papa wished the two others to join them, and the next day Godfrey returned to town. His father remained at

Brinton, without an intermission, the rest of the summer and the whole of the autumn, and Adela had a chance to find out, as she had said, whether he knew she had interfered. But in spite of her chance she never found out. He knew Mrs. Churchley had thrown him over and he knew his daughter rejoiced in it, but he appeared not to have divined the relation between the two facts. It was strange that one of the matters he was clearest about— Adela's secret triumph—should have been just the thing which from this time on justified less and less such a confidence. She was too sorry for him to be consistently glad. She watched his attempts to wind himself up on the subject of shorthorns and drainage, and she favoured to the utmost of her ability his intermittent disposition to make a figure in orchids. She wondered whether they mightn't have a few people at Brinton; but when she mentioned the idea he asked what in the world there would be to attract them. It was a confoundedly stupid house, he remarked—with all respect to *her* cleverness. Beatrice and Muriel were mystified; the prospect of going out immensely had faded so utterly away. They were apparently not to go out at all. Colonel Chart was aimless and bored; he paced up and down and went back to smoking, which was bad for him, and looked drearily out of windows as if on the bare chance that something might arrive. Did he expect Mrs. Churchley to arrive, did he expect her to relent on finding she couldn't live without him? It was Adela's belief that she gave no sign. But the girl thought it really remarkable of her not to have betrayed her ingenious young visitor. Adela's judgement of human nature was perhaps harsh, but she believed that most women, given the various facts, wouldn't have been so forbearing. This lady's conception of the point of honour placed her there in a finer and purer light than had at all originally promised to shine about her.

She meanwhile herself could well judge how heavy her father found the burden of Godfrey's folly and how he was incommoded at having to pay the horrible woman six hundred a year. Doubtless he was having dreadful letters from her; doubtless she threatened them all with hideous exposure. If the matter should be bruited Godfrey's prospects would collapse on the spot. He thought Madrid very charming and curious, but Mrs. Godfrey was in England, so that his father had to face the music. Adela took a dolorous comfort in her mother's being out of that—it would have killed her; but this didn't blind her to the fact that the comfort for her father would perhaps have been greater if he had had some one to talk to about his trouble. He never dreamed of doing so to her, and she felt she couldn't ask him. In the family life he wanted utter silence about it. Early in the winter he went abroad for ten weeks, leaving her with her sisters in the country, where it was not to be denied that at this time existence had very little savour. She half expected her sister-in-law would again descend on her; but the fear wasn't justified, and the quietude of the awful creature seemed really to vibrate with the ring of gold-pieces. There were sure to be extras. Adela winced at the extras. Colonel Chart went to Paris and to Monte Carlo and then to Madrid to see his boy. His daughter had the vision of his perhaps meeting Mrs. Churchley somewhere, since, if she had gone for a year, she would still be on the Continent. If he should meet her perhaps the affair would come on again: she caught herself musing over this. But he brought back no such appearance, and, seeing him after an interval, she was struck afresh with his jilted and wasted air. She didn't like it—she resented it. A little more and she would have said that that was no way to treat so faithful a man.

They all went up to town in March, and on one of the first days of April she saw Mrs. Churchley in the Park. She herself remained apparently invisible to that lady—she herself and Beatrice and Muriel, who sat with her in their mother's old bottle-green landau. Mrs. Churchley, perched higher than ever, rode by without a recognition; but this didn't prevent Adela's going to her before the month was over. As on her great previous occasion she went in the morning, and she again had the good fortune to be admitted. This time, however, her visit was shorter, and a week after making it—the week was a desolation—she addressed to her brother at Madrid a letter containing these words: "I could endure it no longer—I confessed and retracted; I explained to her as well as I could the falsity of what I said to her ten months ago and the benighted purity of my motives for saying it. I besought her to regard it as unsaid, to forgive me, not to despise me too much, to take pity on poor *perfect* papa and come back to him. She was more good-natured than you might have expected—indeed she laughed extravagantly. She had never believed me—it was too absurd; she had only, at the time, disliked me. She found me utterly false—she was very frank with me about this—and she told papa she really thought me horrid. She said she could never live with such a girl, and as I would certainly never marry I must be sent away—in short she quite loathed me. Papa defended me, he refused to sacrifice me, and this led practically to their rupture. Papa gave her up, as it were, for *me*. Fancy the angel, and fancy what I must try to be to him for the rest of his life! Mrs. Churchley can never come back—she's going to marry Lord Dovedale."

THE MIDDLE YEARS

EDITOR'S NOTE

The following pages represent all that Henry James lived to write of a volume of autobiographical reminiscences to which he had given the name of one of his own short stories, The Middle Years. *It was designed to follow on* Notes of a Son and Brother *and to extend to about the same length. The chapters here printed were dictated during the autumn of 1914. They were laid aside for other work toward the end of the year and were not revised by the author. A few quite evident slips have been corrected and the marking of the paragraphs—which he usually deferred till the final revision—has been completed.*

In dictating The Middle Years *he used no notes, and beyond an allusion or two in the unfinished volume itself there is no indication of the course which the book would have taken or the precise period it was intended to cover.*

PERCY LUBBOCK.

I

If the author of this meandering record has noted elsewhere[1] that an event occurring early in 1870 was to mark the end of his youth, he is moved here at once to qualify in one or two respects that emphasis. Everything depends in such a view on what one means by one's youth—so shifting a consciousness is this, and so related at the same time to many different matters. We are never old, that is we never cease easily to be young, for *all* life at the same time: youth is an army, the whole battalion of our faculties and our freshnesses, our passions and our illusions, on a considerably reluctant march into the enemy's country, the country of the general lost freshness; and I think it throws out at least as many stragglers behind as skirmishers ahead—stragglers who often catch up but belatedly with the main body, and even in many a case never catch up at all. Or under another figure it is a book in several volumes, and even at this a mere instalment of the large library of life, with a volume here and there closing, as something in the clap of its covers may assure us, while another remains either completely agape or kept open by a fond finger thrust in between the leaves. A volume, and a most substantial, *had* felt its pages very gravely pressed together before the winter's end that I have spoken of, but a restriction may still bear, and blessedly enough, as I gather from memory, on my sense of the whole year then terminated—a year seen by me now in the light of agitations, explorations, initiations (I scarce know how endearingly enough to name them!) which I should call fairly infantine in their indifference to proportions and aims, had they not still more left with me effects and possessions that even yet lend themselves to estimation.

[1] "Notes of a Son and Brother," 1914.

It was at any rate impossible to have been younger, in spite of whatever inevitable submissions to the rather violent push forward at certain particular points and on lines corresponding with them, than I found myself, from the first day of March 1869, in the face of an opportunity that affected me then and there as the happiest, the most interesting, the most alluring and beguiling, that could ever have opened before a somewhat disabled young man who was about to complete his twenty-sixth year. Treasures of susceptibility, treasures not only unconscious of the remotest approach to exhaustion, but, given the dazzling possibilities, positively and ideally intact, I now recognise—I in fact long ago recognised—on the part of that intensely "reacting" small organism; which couldn't have been in higher spirits or made more inward fuss about the matter if it had come into a property measured not by mere impressions and visions, occasions for play of perception and imagination, mind and soul, but by dollars and "shares," lands and houses or flocks and herds. It is to the account of that immense fantastication that I set down a state of mind so out of proportion to anything it could point to round about save by the vaguest of foolish-looking gestures; and it would perhaps in truth be hard to say whether in the mixture of spirit and sense so determined the fact of innocence or that of intelligence most prevailed. I like to recover this really prodigious flush—as my reader, clearly, must perceive I do; I like fairly to hang about a particular small hour of that momentous March day—which I have glanced at too, I believe, on some other and less separated page than this—for the sake of the extraordinary gage of experience that it seemed on the spot to offer, and that I had but to take straight up: my life, on so complacently near a view as I now treat myself to, having veritably consisted but in the prolongation of that act. I took up the gage, and as I look back the fullest as well as simplest account of the interval till now strikes me as being that I have never, in common honour, let it drop again. And the small hour was just that of my having landed at Liverpool in the gusty, cloudy, overwhelmingly English morning and pursued with immediate intensities of appreciation, as I may call the muffled accompaniment for fear of almost indecently overnaming it, a course which had seated me at a late breakfast in the coffee-room of the old Adelphi Hotel ("Radley's," as I had to deplore its lately having ceased to be dubbed,) and handed me over without a scruple to my fate. This doom of inordinate exposure to appearances, aspects, images, every protrusive item almost, in the great beheld sum of things, I regard in other words as having settled upon me once for all while I observed for instance that in England the plate of buttered muffin and its cover were sacredly set upon the slop-bowl after hot water had been ingenuously poured into the same, and had seen that circumstance in a perfect cloud of accompaniments. I must have had with my tea and my muffin a boiled egg or two and a dab of marmalade, but it was from a far other store of condiments I most liberally helped myself. I was lucidly aware of so gorging—esoterically, as it were, while I drew out the gustatory process; and I must have said in that lost reference to this scene of my dedication which I mentioned above that I was again and again in the aftertime to win back the homeliest notes of the impression, the damp and darksome light washed in from the steep, black, bricky street, the crackle of the strong draught of the British "sea-coal" fire, much more confident of its function, I thought, than the fires I had left, the rustle of the thick, stiff, loudly unfolded and refolded "Times," the incomparable truth to type of the waiter, truth to history, to literature, to poetry, to Dickens, to Thackeray, positively to Smollett, and to Hogarth, to every connection that could help me to appropriate him and his setting, an arrangement of things hanging together with a romantic rightness that had the force of a revelation.

To what end appropriation became thus eager and romance thus easy one could have asked one's self only if the idea of connectibility as stretching away and away hadn't of a sudden taken on such a wealth of suggestion; it represented at once a chain stretching off to heaven knew where, but far into one's future at least, one's possibilities of life, and every link and pulse of which it was going accordingly to be indispensable, besides being delightful and wonderful, to recognise. Recognition, I dare say, was what remained, through the adventure of the months to come, the liveliest principle at work; both as bearing on the already known, on things unforgotten and of a sense intensely cultivated and cherished from my younger time, and on the imagined, the unimagined and the unimaginable, a quantity that divided itself somehow into the double muster of its elements, an endless vista or waiting array, down the middle of which I should inconceivably pass—inconceivably save for being sure of some thrilled arrest, some exchange of assurance and response, at every step. Obviously half the charm, as I can but thinly describe it, of the substantially continuous experience the first passages of which I thus note was in the fact that, immensely moved by it as I was, and having so to deal with it—in the anticipatory way or to the whatevers and wherevers and whenevers within me that should find it in order—I yet felt it in no degree as strange or obscure, baffling or unrecognising on its own side; everything was so far from impenetrable that my most general notion was the very ecstasy of understanding and that really wherever I looked, and still more wherever I pressed, I sank in and in up to my nose. This in particular was of the perfect felicity, that while the fact of difference all round me was immense the embarrassment of it was nil—as if the getting into relation with the least waste had been prepared from so far back that a sort of divine economy now fairly ruled. It was doubtless a part of the total fatuity, and perhaps its sublimest mark, that I knew what everything meant, not simply then but for weeks and months after, and was to know less only with increase of knowledge. That must indeed have been of the essence of the general effect and the particular felicity—only not grotesque because, for want of occasion, not immediately exhibited: a consciousness not other than that of a person abruptly introduced into a preoccupied and animated circle and yet so miraculously aware of the matters conversed about as to need no word of explanation before joining in. To say of such a person that he hadn't lost time would, I knew, be feebly to express his advantage; my likeness to him, at any rate, probably fell short of an absurd one through the chapter of accidents, mostly of the happiest in their way too, which, restraining the personal impulse for me, kept appearances and pretensions down. The feast, as it more and more opened out, was all of the objective, as we have learned so comfortably to say; or at least of its convenient opposite only in so far as this undertook to interpret it for myself alone.

To return at all across the years to the gates of the paradise of the first larger initiations is to be ever so tempted to pass them, to push in again and breathe the air of this, that and the other plot of rising ground particularly associated, for memory and gratitude, with the quickening process. The trouble is that with these sacred spots, to later appreciation, the garden of youth is apt inordinately to bristle, and that one's account of them has to shake them together fairly hard, making a coherent thing of them, to profit by the contribution of each. In speaking of my earliest renewal of the vision of

Europe, if I may give so grand a name to a scarce more than merely enlarged and uplifted gape, I have, I confess, truly to jerk myself over the ground, to wrench myself with violence from memories and images, stages and phases and branching arms, that catch and hold me as I pass them by. Such a matter as my recovery of contact with London for a few weeks, the contact broken off some nine years before, lays so many plausible traps for me that discretion half warns me to stand off the ground and walk round it altogether. I stop my ears to the advice, however, under the pleading reminder that just those days began a business for me that was to go ever so much further than I then dreamed and planted a seed that was, by my own measure, singularly to sprout and flourish—the harvest of which, I almost permit myself to believe, has even yet not all been gathered. I foresee moreover how little I shall be able to resist, throughout these Notes, the force of persuasion expressed in the individual *vivid* image of the past wherever encountered, these images having always such terms of their own, such subtle secrets and insidious arts for keeping us in relation with them, for bribing us by the beauty, the authority, the wonder of their saved intensity. They have saved it, they seem to say to us, from such a welter of death and darkness and ruin that this alone makes a value and a light and a dignity for them, something indeed of an argument that our story, since we attempt to tell one, has lapses and gaps without them. Not to be denied also, over and above this, is the downright pleasure of the illusion yet again created, the *apparent* transfer from the past to the present of the particular combination of things that did at its hour ever so directly operate and that isn't after all then drained of virtue, wholly wasted and lost, for sensation, for participation in the act of life, in the attesting sights, sounds, smells, the illusion, as I say, of the recording senses.

What began, during the springtime of my actual reference, in a couple of dusky ground-floor rooms at number 7 Half-Moon Street, was simply an establishment all in a few days of a personal relation with London that was not of course measurable at the moment—I saw in my bedazzled state of comparative freedom too many other relations ahead, a fairly intoxicated vision of choice and range—but that none the less set going a more intimately inner consciousness, a wheel within the wheels, and led to my departing, the actual, the general incident closed, in possession of a return-ticket "good," as we say, for a longer interval than I could then dream about, and that the first really earnest fumble of after years brought surprisingly to light. I think it must have been the very proportions themselves of the invitation and the interest that kept down, under the immense impression, everything in the nature of calculation and presumption; dark, huge and prodigious the other party to our relation, London's and mine, as I called it, loomed and spread—much too mighty a Goliath for the present in any conceivable ambition even of a fast-growing David. My earlier apprehension, fed at the season as from a thousand outstretched silver spoons—for these all shone to me with that effect of the handsomest hospitality—piled up the monster to such a height that I could somehow only fear him as much as I admired and that his proportions in fact reached away quite beyond my expectation. He was always the great figure of London, and I was for no small time, as the years followed, to be kept at my awe-struck distance for taking him on that sort of trust: I had crept about his ankles, I had glanced adventurously up at his knees, and wasn't the moral for the most part the mere question of whether I should ever be big enough to so much as guess where he stopped?

Odd enough was it, I make out, that I was to feel no wonder of that kind or degree play in the coming time over such other social aspects, such superficially more colourable scenes as I paid, in repetition as frequent as possible, my respects and my compliments to: they might meet me with wreathed smiles and splendid promises and deep divinations of my own desire, a thousand graces and gages, in fine, that I couldn't pretend to have picked up within the circle, however experimentally widened, of which Half-Moon Street was the centre, and nothing therefore could have exceeded the splendour of these successive and multiplied assurances. What it none the less infinitely beguiles me to recognise to-day is that such exhibitions, for all their greater direct radiance, and still more for all their general implication of a store of meaning and mystery and beauty that they alone, from example to example, from prodigy to prodigy, had to open out, left me comparatively little crushed by the impression of their concerning me further than my own action perhaps could make good. It was as if I had seen that all there was for me of these great things I should sooner or later take; the amount would be immense, yet, as who should say, all on the same plane and the same connection, the æsthetic, the "artistic," the romantic in the looser sense, or in other words in the air of the passions of the intelligence. What other passions of a deeper strain, whether personal or racial, and thereby more superstitiously importunate, I must have felt involved in the question of an effective experience of English life I was doubtless then altogether unprepared to say; it probably came, however, I seem actually to make out, very much to this particular perception, exactly, that any penetration of the London scene would *be* experience after a fashion that an exercise of one's "mere intellectual curiosity" wherever else wouldn't begin to represent, glittering as the rewards to such curiosity amid alien peoples of genius might thoroughly appear. On the other hand it was of course going to be nothing less than a superlative help that one would have but to reach out straight and in the full measure of one's passion for these rewards, to find one's self carried all the way by one's active, one's contemplative concern with them—this delightful affair, fraught with increase of light, of joy and wonder, of possibilities of adventure for the mind, in fine, inevitably exhausting the relation.

II

Let me not here withal appear to pretend to say how far I then foresaw myself likely to proceed, as it were, with the inimitable France and the incomparable Italy; my real point is altogether in the simple fact that they hovered before me, even in their scrappy foretastes, to a great effect of ease and inspiration, whereas I shouldn't at all have resented the charge of fairly hiding behind the lowly door of Mr. Lazarus Fox—so unmistakeably did it open into complications tremendous. This excellent man, my Half-Moon Street landlord—I surrender, I can't keep away from him—figures to me now as but one of the thousand forms of pressure in the collective assault, but he couldn't have been more carefully chosen for his office had he consciously undertaken to express to me in a concentrated manner most of the things I was "after." The case was rather indeed perhaps that he himself by his own mere perfection put me up to much of what I should most confidently look for, and that the right lines of observation and enjoyment, of local and social contact, as I may call it, were most of all those that started out from him and came back to him. It was as if nothing I saw could have done without him, as if nothing he was could have done without everything else. The very quarters I occupied under his protection happened, for that matter, to swarm—as I estimated swarming—with intensities of suggestion—aware as I now encourage myself to become that the first note of the numberless reverberations I was to pick up in the aftertime had definitely been struck for me as under the wave of his conducting little wand. He flourished it modestly enough, ancient worthy of an immemorial order that he was— old pensioned servant, of course, of a Cumberland (as I believe) family, a kind, slim, celibate, informing and informed member of which occupied his second floor apartments; a friend indeed whom I had met on the very first occasion of my sallying forth from Morley's Hotel in Trafalgar Square to dine at a house of sustaining, of inspiring hospitality in the Kensington quarter. Succumbing thus to my tangle of memories, from which I discern no escape, I recognise further that if the endlessly befriending Charles Nortons introduced me to Albert Rutson, and Albert Rutson introduced me to his feudal retainer, so it was in no small degree through the confidence borrowed from the latter's interest in the decent appearance I should make, an interest of a consistency not to have been prefigured by any at all like instance in my past, that I so far maintained my dizzy balance as to be able to ascend to the second floor under the thrill of sundry invitations to breakfast. I dare say it is the invitations to breakfast that hold me at this moment by their spell—so do they breathe to me across the age the note of a London world that we have left far behind; in consequence of which I the more yearningly steal back to it, as on sneaking tiptoe, and shut myself up there without interference. It is embalmed in disconnections, in differences, that I cultivate a free fancy for pronouncing advantageous to it: sunk already was the shaft by which I should descend into the years, and my inspiration is in touching as many as possible of the points of the other tradition, retracing as many as possible of the features of the old face, eventually to be blurred again even before my own eyes, and with the materials for a portrait thereby accessible but to those who were present up to the time of the change.

I don't pretend to date this change which still allows me to catch my younger observation and submission at play on the far side of it; I make it fall into the right perspective, however, I think, when I place it where I began to shudder before a confidence, not to say an impudence, of diminution in the aspects by which the British capital differed so from those of all the foreign together as to present throughout the straight contradiction to them. That straight contradiction, testifying invaluably at every turn, had been from far back the thing, romantically speaking, to clutch and keep the clue and the logic of; thanks to it the whole picture, every element, objects and figures, background and actors, nature and art, hung consummately together, appealing in their own light and under their own law—interesting ever in every case by instituting comparisons, sticking on the contrary to their true instinct and suggesting only contrast. They were the *opposite*, the assured, the absolute, the unashamed, in respect to whatever might be of a generally similar intention elsewhere: this was their dignity, their beauty and their strength—to look back on which is to wonder if one didn't quite consciously tremble, before the exhibition, for any menaced or mitigated symptom in it.

I honestly think one did, even in the first flushes of recognition, more or less so tremble; I remember at least that in spite of such disconcertments, such dismays, as certain of the most thoroughly Victorian *choses vues* originally treated me to, something yet deeper and finer than observation admonished me to like them just as they were, or at least not too fatuously to dislike—since it somehow glimmered upon me that if they had lacked their oddity, their monstrosity, as it even might be, their unabashed insular conformity, other things that belong to them, as they belong to these, might have loomed less large and massed less thick, which effect was wholly to be deprecated. To catch that secret, I make out the more I think of it, was to have perhaps the smokiest, but none the less the steadiest, light to walk by; the "clue," as I have called it, was to be one's appreciation of an England that should turn its back directly enough, and without fear of doing it too much, on examples and ideas not strictly homebred—since she did her own sort of thing with such authority and was even then to be noted as sometimes trying other people's with a *kind* of disaster not recorded, at the worst, among themselves.

I must of course disavow pretending to have read this vivid philosophy into my most immediate impressions, and I may in fact perhaps not claim to have been really aware of its seed till a considerable time had passed, till apprehensions and reflections had taken place in quantity, immeasurable quantity, so to speak, and a great stir-up of the imagination been incurred. Undoubtedly is it in part the new—that is, more strictly, the elder—acuteness that I touch all the prime profit with; I didn't know at the time either how much appearances were all the while in the melting-pot or what wealth of reaction on them I was laying up. I cherish, for love of the unbroken interest, all the same, the theory of certain then positive and effective prefigurements, because it leaves me thus free for remarking that I knew where I was, as I may put it, from the moment I saw the state of the London to come brought down with the weight of her abdication of her genius. It not unnaturally may be said that it hasn't been till to-day that we *see* her genius in its fulness—throwing up in a hundred lights, matters we practically acknowledge, such a plastic side as we had never dreamed she possessed. The genius of accommodation is what we had last expected of her—accommodation to anything but her portentous self, for in *that* connection she was ever remarkable; and certainly the air of the generalised, the emulous smart modern capital has come to be written upon her larger and larger even while we look.

The unaccommodating and unaccommodated city remains none the less closely consecrated to one's fondest notion of her—the city too indifferent, too proud, too unaware, too stupid even if one will, to enter any lists that involved her moving from her base and that thereby, when one approached her from the alien *positive* places (I don't speak of the American, in those days too negative to be related at all) enjoyed the enormous "pull," for making her impression, of ignoring everything but her own perversities and then of driving these home with an emphasis not to be gainsaid. Since she didn't emulate, as I have termed it, so she practised her own arts altogether, and both these ways and these consequences were in the flattest opposition (*that* was the happy point!) to foreign felicities or foreign standards, so that the effect in every case was of the straightest reversal of them—with black for the foreign white and white for the foreign black, wet for the foreign dry and dry for the foreign wet, big for the foreign small and small for the foreign big: I needn't extend the catalogue. *Her* idiosyncrasy was never in the least to have been inferred or presumed; it could only, in general, make the outsider provisionally gape. She sat thus imperturbable in her felicities, and if that is how, remounting the stream of time, I like most to think of her, this is because if her interest is still undeniable—as that of overgrown things goes—it has yet lost its fineness of quality. Phenomena may be interesting, thank goodness, without being phenomena of elegant expression or of any other form of restless smartness, and when once type is strong, when once it plays up from deep sources, every show of its sincerity delivers us a message and we hang, to real suspense, on its continuance of energy, on its again and yet again consistently acquitting itself. So it keeps in tune, and, as the French adage says, *c'est le ton qui fait la chanson*. The mid-Victorian London was sincere—that was a vast virtue and a vast appeal; the contemporary is sceptical, and most so when most plausible; the turn of the tide could verily be fixed to an hour—the hour at which the new plausibility began to exceed the old sincerities by so much as a single sign. They could truly have been arrayed face to face, I think, for an attentive eye—and I risk even saying that my own, bent upon them, as was to come to pass, with a habit of anxiety that I should scarce be able to overstate, had its unrecorded penetrations, its alarms and recoveries, even perhaps its very lapses of faith, though always redeemed afresh by still fonder fanaticisms, to a pitch that shall perhaps present itself, when they expose it all the way, as that of tiresome extravagance. Exposing it all the way is none the less, I see, exactly what I plot against it—or, otherwise expressed, in favour of the fine truth of history, so far as a throb of that awful pulse has been matter of one's own life; in favour too of the mere returns derivable from more inordinate curiosity. These Notes would enjoy small self-respect, I think, if that principle, not to call it that passion, didn't almost furiously ride them.

III

I was at any rate in the midst of sincerities enough, sincerities of emphasis and "composition"; perversities, idiosyncrasies, incalculabilities, delightful all as densities at first insoluble, delightful even indeed as so much mere bewilderment and shock. When was the shock, I ask myself as I look back, not so deadened by the general atmospheric richness as not to melt more or less immediately into some succulence for the mind, something that could feed the historic sense almost to sweetness? I don't mean that it was a shock to be invited to breakfast—there were stronger ones than that; but was in fact the *trait de mœurs* that disconnected me with most rapidity and intensity from all I had left on the other side of the sea. To be so disconnected, for the time, and in the most insidious manner, was above all what I had come out for, and every appearance that might help it was to be artfully and gratefully cultivated. I recollect well how many of these combined as I sat at quite punctual fried sole and marmalade in the comparatively disengaged sitting-room of the second floor—the occupancy of the first has remained vague to me; disengaged from the mantle of gloom the folds of which draped most heavily the feet of the house, as it were, and thereby promoted in my own bower the chronic dusk favourable to mural decoration consisting mainly of framed and glazed "coloured" excisions from Christmas numbers of the Illustrated London News that had been at their hour quite modern miracles. Was it for that matter into a sudden splendour of the modern that I ascendingly emerged under the hospitality of my kind fellow-tenant, or was it rather into the fine classicism of a bygone age, as literature and the arts had handed down that memory? Such were the questions whisked at every turn under my nose and reducing me by their obscure charm but to bewildered brooding, I fear, when I should have been myself, to repay these attentions, quite forward and informing and affirmative.

There were eminent gentlemen, as I was sure they could only be, to "meet" and, alas, awfully to interrogate me—for vivid has remained to me, as the best of my bewilderment, the strangeness of finding that I could be of interest to *them*: not indeed to call it rather the proved humiliation of my impotence. My identity for myself was *all* in my sensibility to their own exhibition, with not a scrap left over for a personal show; which made it as inconvenient as it was queer that I should be treated as a specimen and have in the most unexpected manner to prove that I was a good one. I knew myself the very worst conceivable, but how to give to such other persons a decent or coherent reason for my being so required more presence of mind than I could in the least muster—the consequence of which failure had to be for me, I fear, under all that confused first flush, rather an abject acceptance of the air of imbecility. There were, it appeared, things of interest taking place in America, and I had had, in this absurd manner, to come to England to learn it: I had had over there on the ground itself no conception of any such matter—nothing of the smallest interest, by any perception of mine, as I suppose I should still blush to recall, had taken place in America since the War. How *could* anything, I really wanted to ask—anything comparable, that is, to what was taking place under my eyes in Half-Moon Street and at dear softly presiding Rutson's table of talk. It doubtless essentially belonged to the exactly right type and tone and general figure of my fellow-breakfasters from the Temple, from the Home Office, the Foreign Office, the House of Commons, from goodness knew what other scarce discernible Olympian altitudes, it belonged to the very cut of their hair and their waistcoats and their whiskers—for it was still more or less a whiskered age—that they should desire from me much distinctness about General Grant's first cabinet, upon the formation of which the light of the newspaper happened then to beat; yet at the same time that I asked myself if it was to such cold communities, such flat frustrations as were so proposed, that I had sought to lift my head again in European air, I found the crisis enriched by sundry other apprehensions.

They melted together in it to that increase of savour I have already noted, yet leaving me vividly admonished that the blankness of my mind as to the Washington candidates relegated me to some class unencountered as yet by any one of my conversers, a class only not perfectly ridiculous because perfectly insignificant. Also that politics walked abroad in England, so that one might supremely bump against them, as much as, by my fond impression, they took their exercise in America but through the back streets and the ways otherwise untrodden and the very darkness of night; that further all lively attestations were *ipso facto* interesting, and that finally and in the supreme degree, the authenticity of whatever one was going to learn in the world would probably always have for its sign that one got it at some personal cost. To this generalisation mightn't one even add that in proportion as the cost was great, or became fairly excruciating, the lesson, the value acquired would probably be a thing to treasure? I remember really going so far as to wonder if any act of acquisition of the life-loving, life-searching sort that most appealed to me wouldn't mostly be fallacious if unaccompanied by that tag of the price paid in personal discomfort, in some self-exposure and some none too impossible consequent discomfiture, for the sake of it. Didn't I even on occasion mount to the very height of seeing it written that these bad moments were the downright consecration of knowledge, that is of perception and, essentially, of exploration, always dangerous and treacherous, and so might afterwards come to figure to memory, each in its order, as the silver nail on the wall of the temple where the trophy is hung up? All of which remark, I freely grant, is a great ado about the long since so bedimmed little Half-Moon Street breakfasts, and is moreover quite wide of the mark if suggesting that the joys of recognition, those of imaginatively, of projectively fitting in and fitting out every piece in the puzzle and every recruit to the force of a further understanding weren't in themselves a most bustling and cheering business.

It was bustling at least, assuredly, if not quite always in the same degree exhilarating, to breakfast out at all, as distinguished from lunching, without its being what the Harvard scene made of it, one of the incidents of "boarding"; it was association at a jump with the ghosts of Byron and Sheridan and Scott and Moore and Lockhart and Rogers and *tutti quanti*—as well as the exciting note of a social order in which everyone wasn't hurled straight, with the momentum of rising, upon an office or a store. The mere vision in numbers of persons embodying and in various ways sharply illustrating a clear alternative to that passivity told a tale that would be more and more worth the reading with every turn of the page. So at all events I fantasticated while harassed by my necessity to weave into my general tapestry every thread that would conduce to a pattern, and so the thread for instance of the great little difference of my literally never having but once "at home" been invited to breakfast on types as well as on toast and its accessories could suggest an effect of silk or silver when absolutely dangled before me. That single occasion at home came back in a light that fairly brought tears to my eyes, for it was touching now to the last wanness that the lady of the winter morn of the Massachusetts Sabbath, one of those, as I recover it, of 1868, to reach whose board we had waded through snowdrifts, had been herself fondling a reminiscence, though I can scarce imagine supposing herself to offer for our consumption any other type than her own. It was for that matter but the sweet staleness of her reminiscence that made her a type, and I remember how it had had to do thereby all the work: *she*, of an age to reach so considerably back, had breakfasted out, in London, and with Mr. Rogers himself—that was the point; which I am bound to say did for the hour and on that spot supply richness of reference enough. And I am caught up, I find, in the very act of this claim for my prior scantness of experience by a memory that makes it not a little less perfect and which is oddly enough again associated with a struggle, on an empty stomach, through the massed New England whiteness of the prime Sunday hour. I still cherish the vision, which couldn't then have faded from me, of my having, during the age of innocence—I mean of my own—breakfasted with W. D. Howells, insidious disturber and fertiliser of that state in me, to "meet" Bayard Taylor and Arthur Sedgwick all in the Venetian manner, the delightful Venetian manner which toward the later 'sixties draped any motion on our host's part as with a habit still appropriate. *He* had risen that morning under the momentum of his but recently concluded consular term in Venice, where margin, if only that of the great loungeable piazza, had a breadth, and though Sedgwick and I had rather, as it were, to take the jump standing, this was yet under the inspiration of feeling the case most special. Only it had *been* Venetian, snow-shoes and all; I had stored it sacredly away as not American at all, and was of course to learn in Half-Moon Street how little it had been English either.

What must have seemed to me of a fine international mixture, during those weeks, was my thrilling opportunity to sit one morning, beside Mrs. Charles Norton's tea-urn, in Queen's Gate Terrace, opposite to Frederic Harrison, eminent to me at the moment as one of the subjects of Matthew Arnold's early fine banter, one of his too confidently roaring "young lions" of the periodical press. Has any gilding ray since that happy season rested here and there with the sovereign charm of interest, of drollery, of felicity and infelicity taken on by scattered selected objects in that writer's bright critical dawn?—an element in which we had the sense of sitting gratefully bathed, so that we fairly took out our young minds and dabbled and soaked them in it as we were to do again in no other. The beauty was thus at such a rate that people had references, and that a reference was then, to my mind, whether in a person or an object, the most glittering, the most becoming ornament possible, a style of decoration one seemed likely to perceive figures here and there, whether animate or not, quite groan under the accumulation and the weight of. One had scarcely met it before—that I now understood; at the same time that there was perhaps a wan joy in one's never having missed it, by all appearance, having on the contrary ever instinctively caught it, on the least glimmer of its presence. Even when present, or what in the other time I had taken for present, it had been of the thinnest, whereas all about me hereafter it would be by all appearance almost glutinously thick—to the point even of one's on occasion sticking fast in it; that is finding intelligibility smothered in quantity. I lost breath in fact, no doubt, again and again, with this latter increase, but was to go on and on for a long time before any first glimmer of reaction against so special a source of interest. It attached itself to objects often, I saw, by no merit or virtue—above all, repeatedly, by no "cleverness"—of their own, but just by the luck of history, by the action of multiplicity of circumstance. Condemned the human particle "over here" was to *live* on whatever terms, in thickness—instead of being free, comparatively, or as I at once ruefully and exquisitely found myself, only to feel and to think in it. Ruefully because there were clearly a thousand contacts and sensations, of the strong direct order, that one lost by not so living; exquisitely because of the equal number of immunities and independences, blest independences of perception and judgment, blest liberties of range for the intellectual adventure, that accrued by the same stroke. These at least had the advantage, one of the most distinguished conceivable, that when enjoyed with a certain intensity they might produce the illusion of the other intensity, that of being involved in the composition and the picture itself, in the situations, the complications, the circumstances, admirable and dreadful; while no corresponding illusion, none making for the ideal play of reflection, conclusion, comparison, however one should incline to appraise the luxury, seemed likely to attend the immersed or engaged condition.

Whatever fatuity might at any rate have resided in these complacencies of view, I made them my own with the best conscience in the world, and I meet them again quite to extravagance of interest wherever on the whole extent of the scene my retrospect sets me down. It wasn't in the least at the same time that encountered celebrities only thus provoked the shifting play of my small lamp, and this too even though they were easily celebrated, by my measure, and though from the very first I owed an individual here and there among them, as was highly proper, the benefit of impression at the highest pitch. On the great supporting and enclosing scene itself, the big generalised picture, painted in layer upon layer and tone upon tone, one's fancy was all the while feeding; objects and items, illustrations and aspects might perpetually overlap or mutually interfere, but never without leaving consistency the more marked and character the more unmistakeable. The place, the places, bristled so for every glance with expressive particulars, that I really conversed with them, at happy moments, more than with the figures that moved in them, which affected me so often as but submissive articles of furniture, "put in" by an artist duly careful of effect and yet duly respectful of proportion. The great impression was doubtless no other then and there than what it is under every sky and before every scene that remind one afresh, at the given moment, of all the ways in which producing causes and produced creatures correspond and interdepend; but I think I must have believed at that time that these cross references kept up their game in the English air with a frankness and a good faith that kept the process, in all probability, the most traceable of its kind on the globe.

What was the secret of the force of that suggestion?—which was not, I may say, to be invalidated, to my eyes, by the further observation of cases and conditions. Was it that the enormous "pull" enjoyed at every point of the general surface the stoutness of the underlying belief in what was behind all surfaces?—so that the particular visible, audible, palpable fact, however small and subsidiary, was incomparably absolute, or had, so to speak, such a conscience and a confidence, such an absence of reserve and latent doubts about itself, as was not elsewhere to be found. Didn't such elements as that represent, in the heart of things, possibilities of scepticism, of mockery, of irony, of the return of the matter, whatever it might be, on itself, by some play or other of the questioning spirit, the spirit therefore weakening to entire comfort of affirmations? Didn't I see that humour itself, which might seem elsewhere corrosive and subversive, was, as an English faculty, turned outward altogether and never turned inward?—by which convenient circumstance subversion, or in other words alteration and variation were not promoted. Such truths were wondrous things to make out in such connections as my experience was then, and for no small time after, to be confined to; but I positively catch myself listening to them, even with my half-awakened ears, as if they had been all so many sermons of the very stones of London. *There*, to come back to it, was exactly the force with which these stones were to build me capaciously round: I invited them, I besought them, to say all they would, and—to return to my figure of a while back—it was soon so thoroughly as if they had understood that, once having begun, they were to keep year after year fairly chattering to me. Many of these pages, I fondly foresee, must consist but of the record of their chatter. What was most of all happening, I take it, was that under an absurd special stress I was having, as who should say, to improvise a local medium and to arrange a local consciousness. Against my due appropriation of those originally closest at my hand inevitable accidents had conspired—and, to conclude in respect to all this, if a considerable time was to be wanted, in the event, for ideal certainty of adjustment, half the terms required by this could then put forth the touching plea that they had quite achingly waited.

IV

It may perhaps seem strange that the soil should have been watered by such an incident as Mr. Lazarus Fox's reply, in the earliest rich dusk, to my inquiry as to whither, while I occupied his rooms, I had best betake myself most regularly for my dinner: "Well, there is the Bath Hotel, sir, a very short walk away, where I should think you would be very comfortable indeed. Mr. So-and-So dines at his club, sir—but there is also the Albany in Piccadilly, to which I believe many gentlemen go." I think I measured on the spot "all that it took" to make my friend most advisedly—for it was clearly what he did—see me seated in lone state, for my evening meal, at the heavy mahogany of the stodgy little hotel that in those days and for long after occupied the north-west corner of Arlington Street and to which, in common with many compatriots, I repeatedly resorted during the years immediately following. We *suffered*, however, on those occasions, the unmitigated coffee-room of Mr. Fox's prescription—it was part of a strange inevitability, a concomitant of necessary shelter and we hadn't at least gone forth to invoke its austere charm. I tried it, in that singular way, at the hour I speak of—and I well remember forecasting the interest of a social and moral order in which it could be supposed of me that, having tried it once, I should sublimely try it again. My success in doing so would indeed have been sublime, but a finer shade of the quality still attached somehow to my landlord's confidence in it; and this was one of the threads that, as I have called them, I was to tuck away for future picking-up again and unrolling. I fell back on the Albany, which long ago passed away and which I seem to have brushed with a touch of reminiscence in some anticipation of the present indulgence that is itself quite ancient history. It was a small eating-house of the very old English tradition, as I then supposed at least, just opposite the much greater establishment of the same name, which latter it had borrowed, and I remember wondering whether the tenants of the classic chambers, the beadle-guarded cluster of which was impressive even to the deprecated approach, found their conception of the "restaurant"—we still pronounced it in the French manner—met by the small compartments, narrow as horse-stalls, formed by the high straight backs of hard wooden benches and accommodating respectively two pairs of feeders, who were thus so closely face to face as fairly to threaten with knife and fork each others' more forward features.

The scene was sordid, the arrangements primitive, the detail of the procedure, as it struck me, well-nigh of the rudest; yet I remember rejoicing in it all—as one indeed might perfectly rejoice in the juiciness of joints and the abundance of accessory pudding; for I said to myself under every shock and at the hint of every savour that this was what it was for an exhibition to reek with local colour, and one could dispense with a napkin, with a crusty roll, with room for one's elbows or one's feet, with an immunity from intermittence of the "plain boiled," much better than one could dispense with that. There were restaurants galore even at that time in New York and in Boston, but I had never before had to do with an eating-house and had not yet seen the little old English world of Dickens, let alone of the ever-haunting Hogarth, of Smollett and of Boswell, drenched with such a flood of light. As one sat there one *understood*; one drew out the severe séance not to stay the assault of precious conspiring truths, not to break the current of in-rushing telltale suggestion. Every face was a documentary scrap, half a dozen broken words to piece with half a dozen others, and so on and on; every sound was strong, whether rich and fine or only queer and coarse; everything in this order drew a positive sweetness from never being—whatever else it was—gracelessly flat. The very rudeness was ripe, the very commonness was conscious—that is not related to mere other forms of the same, but to matters as different as possible, into which it shaded off and off or up and up; the image in fine was organic, rounded and complete, as definite as a Dutch picture of low life hung on a museum wall. "Low" I say in respect to the life; but that was the point for me, that whereas the smartness and newness beyond the sea supposedly disavowed the low, they did so but thinly and vainly, falling markedly short of the high; which the little boxed and boiled Albany attained to some effect of, after a fashion of its own, just by having its so thoroughly appreciable note-value in a scheme of manners. It was imbedded, so to speak, in the scheme, and it borrowed lights, it borrowed even glooms, from so much neighbouring distinction. The places across the sea, as they to my then eyes faintly after-glowed, had no impinging borders but those of the desert to borrow *from*. And if it be asked of me whether all the while I insist, for demonstration of the complacency with which I desire to revert, on not regretting the disappearance of such too long surviving sordidries as those I have evoked, I can but answer that blind emotion, in whichever sense directed, has nothing to say to the question and that the sense of what we just *could* confidently live by at a given far-away hour is a simple stout fact of relief.

Relief, again, I say, from the too enormous present accretions and alternatives—which we witlessly thought so innumerable then, which we artlessly found so much of the interest of *in* an immeasurable multiplicity and which I now feel myself thus grope for ghostly touch of in the name, neither more nor less, of poetic justice. I wasn't doubtless at the time so very sure, after all, of the comparative felicity of our state, that of the rare *moment* for the fond fancy—I doubtless even a bit greedily missed certain quantities, not to call them certain qualities, here and there, and the best of my actual purpose is to make amends for that blasphemy. There isn't a thing I can imagine having missed that I don't quite ache to miss again; and it remains at all events an odd stroke that, having of old most felt the thrill of the place in its mighty muchness, I have lived to adore it backward for its sweet simplicity. I find myself in fact at the present writing only too sorry when not able to minimise conscientiously this, that or the other of the old sources of impression. The thing is indeed admirably possible in a *general* way, though much of the exhibition was none the less undeniably, was absolutely large: how can I for instance recall the great cab-rank, mainly formed of delightful hansoms, that stretched along Piccadilly from the top of the Green Park unendingly down, without having to take it for unsurpassably modern and majestic? How can I think—I select my examples at hazard—of the "run" of the more successful of Mr. Robertson's comedies at the "dear little old" Prince of Wales's Theatre in Tottenham Court Road as anything less than one of the wonders of our age? How, by the same token, can I not lose myself still more in the glory of a time that was to watch the drawn-out procession of Henry Irving's Shakespearean splendours at the transcendent Lyceum? or how, in the same general line, not recognise that to live through the extravagant youth of the æsthetic era, whether as embodied in the then apparently inexhaustible

74

vein of the Gilbert and Sullivan operas or as more monotonously expressed in those "last words" of the *raffiné* that were chanted and crooned in the damask-hung temple of the Grosvenor Gallery, was to seem privileged to such immensities as history would find left to her to record but with bated breath?

These latter triumphs of taste, however, though lost in the abysm now, had then a good many years to wait and I alight for illustrative support of my present mild thesis on the comparative humility, say, of the inward aspects, in a large measure, of the old National Gallery, where memory mixes for me together so many elements of the sense of an antique world. The great element was of course that I well-nigh incredibly stood again in the immediate presence of Titian and Rembrandt, of Rubens and Paul Veronese, and that the cup of sensation was thereby filled to overflowing; but I look at it to-day as concomitantly warm and closed-in and, as who should say, cosy that the ancient order and contracted state and thick-coloured dimness, all unconscious of rearrangements and reversals, blighting new lights and invidious shattering comparisons, still prevailed and kept contemplation comfortably confused and serenely superstitious, when not indeed at its sharpest moments quite fevered with incoherences. The place looks to me across the half century richly dim, yet at the same time both perversely plain and heavily violent—violent through indifference to the separations and selections that have become a tribute to modern nerves; but I cherish exactly those facts of benightedness, seeming as they do to have positively and blessedly conditioned the particular sweetness of wonder with which I haunted the Family of Darius, the Bacchus and Ariadne, or the so-called portrait of Ariosto. Could one in those days feel anything with force, whether for pleasure or for pain, without feeling it as an immense little act or event of life, and as therefore taking place on a scene and in circumstances scarce at all to be separated from its own sense and impact?—so that to recover it is to recover the whole medium, the material pressure of things, and find it most marked for preservation as an aspect, even, distinguishably, a "composition."

What a composition, for instance again I am capable at this hour of exclaiming, the conditions of felicity in which I became aware, one afternoon during a renewed gape before the Bacchus and Ariadne, first that a little gentleman beside me and talking with the greatest vivacity to another gentleman was extremely remarkable, second that he had the largest and most *chevelu* auburn head I had ever seen perched on a scarce perceptible body, third that I held some scrap of a clue to his identity, which couldn't fail to be eminent, fourth that this tag of association was with nothing less than a small photograph sent me westward across the sea a few months before, and fifth that the sitter for the photograph had been the author of Atalanta in Calydon and Poems and Ballads! I thrilled, it perfectly comes back to me, with the prodigy of this circumstance that I should be admiring Titian in the same breath with Mr. Swinburne—that is in the same breath in which *he* admired Titian and in which I also admired *him*, the whole constituting on the spot between us, for appreciation, that is for mine, a fact of intercourse, such a fact as could stamp and colour the whole passage ineffaceably, and this even though the more illustrious party to it had within the minute turned off and left me shaken. I was shaken, but I was satisfied—that was the point; I didn't ask more to interweave another touch in my pattern, and as I once more gather in the impression I am struck with my having deserved truly as many of the like as possible. I was welcome to them, it may well be said, on such easy terms—and yet I ask myself whether, after all, it didn't take on my own part some doing, as we nowadays say, to make them so well worth having. They themselves took, I even at the time felt, little enough trouble for it, and the virtue of the business was repeatedly, no doubt, a good deal more in what I brought than in what I took.

I apply this remark indeed to those extractions of the quintessence that had for their occasion either one's more undirected though never fruitless walks and wanderings or one's earnest, one's positively pious approach to whatever consecrated ground or shrine of pilgrimage that might be at the moment in order. There was not a regular prescribed "sight" that I during those weeks neglected—I remember haunting the museums in especial, though the South Kensington was then scarce more than embryonic, with a sense of duty and of excitement that I was never again to know combined in equal measure, I think, and that it might really have taken some element of personal danger to account for. There *was* the element, in a manner, to season the cup with sharpness—the danger, all the while, that my freedom might be brief and my experience broken, that I was under the menace of uncertainty and subject in fine to interruption. The fact of having been so long gravely unwell sufficed by itself to keep apprehension alive; it was our idea, or at least quite intensely mine, that what I was doing, could I but put it through, would be intimately good for me—only the putting it through was the difficulty, and I sometimes faltered by the way. This makes now for a general air on the part of all the objects of vision that I recover, and almost as much in those of accidental encounter as in the breathlessly invoked, of being looked at for the last time and giving out their message and story as with the still, collected passion of an only chance. This feeling about them, not to say, as I might have imputed it, *in* them, wonderfully helped, as may be believed, the extraction of quintessences—which sprang at me of themselves, for that matter, out of any appearance that confessed to the least value in the compound, the least office in the harmony. If the commonest street-vista was a fairly heart-shaking contributive image, if the incidents of the thick renascent light anywhere, and the perpetual excitement of never knowing, between it and the historic and determined gloom, which was which and which one would most "back" for the general outcome and picture, so the great sought-out compositions, the Hampton Courts and the Windsors, the Richmonds, the Dulwiches, even the very Hampstead Heaths and Putney Commons, to say nothing of the Towers, the Temples, the Cathedrals and the strange penetrabilities of the City, ranged themselves like the rows of great figures in a sum, an amount immeasurably huge, that one would draw on if not quite as long as one lived, yet as soon as ever one should seriously get to work. That, to a tune of the most beautiful melancholy—at least as I catch it again now—was the way all values came out: they were charged somehow with a useability the most immediate, the most urgent, and which, I seemed to see, would keep me restless till I should have done something of my very own with them.

This was indeed perhaps what most painted them over with the admonitory appeal: there were truly moments at which they seemed not to answer for it that I should get all the good of them, and the finest—what I was so extravagantly, so fantastically after—unless I could somehow at once indite my sonnet and prove my title. The difficulty was all in there being so much of them—I might myself have been less restless if they could only have been less vivid. This they absolutely declined at any moment and in any connection to be, and it was ever so long till they abated a jot of the refusal. Thereby, in consequence, as may easily be judged, they were to keep me in alarms to which my measures practically taken, my catastrophes anxiously averted, remained not quite proportionate. I recall a most interesting young man who had been my shipmate on the homeward-bound "China," shortly before—I could go at length into my reasons for having been so struck with him, but I forbear—who, on our talking, to my intense trepidation of curiosity, of where I might advisedly "go" in London, let me know that he always went to Craven Street Strand, where bachelor lodgings were highly convenient, and whence I in fact then saw them flush at me over the cold grey sea with an authenticity almost fierce. I didn't in the event, as has been seen, go to Craven Street for rooms, but I did go, on the very first occasion, for atmosphere, neither more nor less—the young man of the ship, building so much better than he knew, had guaranteed me such a rightness of that; and it belongs to this reminiscence, for the triviality of which I should apologize did I find myself at my present pitch capable of apologizing for anything, that I had on the very spot there one of those hallucinations as to the precious effect dreadful to lose and yet impossible to render which interfused the æsthetic dream in presence of its subject with the mortal drop of despair (as I should insist at least didn't the despair itself seem to have acted here as the preservative). The precious effect in the case of Craven Street was that it absolutely reeked, to my fond fancy, with associations born of the particular ancient piety embodied in one's private altar to Dickens; and that this upstart little truth alone would revel in explanations that I should for the time have feverishly to forego. The exquisite matter was not the identification with the scene of special shades or names; it was just that the whole Dickens procession marched up and down, the whole Dickens world looked out of its queer, quite sinister windows—for it was the socially sinister Dickens, I am afraid, rather than the socially encouraging or confoundingly comic who still at that moment was most apt to meet me with his reasons. Such a reason was just that look of the inscrutable riverward street, packed to blackness with accumulations of suffered experience, these, indescribably, disavowed and confessed at one and the same time, and with the fact of its blocked old Thames-side termination, a mere fact of more oppressive enclosure now, telling all sorts of vague loose stories about it.

V

Why, however, should I pick up so small a crumb from that mere brief first course at a banquet of initiation which was in the event to prolong itself through years and years?—unless indeed as a scrap of a specimen, chosen at hazard, of the prompt activity of a process by which my intelligence afterwards came to find itself more fed, I think, than from any other source at all, or, for that matter, from all other sources put together. A hundred more suchlike modest memories breathe upon me, each with its own dim little plea, as I turn to face them, but my idea is to deal somehow more conveniently with the whole gathered mass of my subsequent impressions in this order, a fruitage that I feel to have been only too abundantly stored. Half a dozen of those of a larger and more immediate dignity, incidents more particularly of the rather invidiously so-called social contact, pull my sleeve as I pass; but the long, backward-drawn train of the later life drags them along with it, lost and smothered in its spread—only one of them stands out or remains over, insisting on its place and hour, its felt distinguishability. To this day I feel again *that* roused emotion, my unsurpassably prized admission to the presence of the great George Eliot, whom I was taken to see, by one of the kind door-opening Norton ladies, by whom Mrs. Lewes's guarded portal at North Bank appeared especially penetrable, on a Sunday afternoon of April '69. Later occasions, after a considerable lapse, were not to overlay the absolute face-value, as I may call it, of all the appearances then and there presented me—which were taken home by a young spirit almost abjectly grateful, at any rate all devoutly prepared, for them. I find it idle even to wonder what "place" the author of Silas Marner and Middlemarch may be conceived to have in the pride of our literature—so settled and consecrated in the individual range of view is many such a case free at last to find itself, free after ups and downs, after fluctuations of fame or whatever, which have divested judgment of any relevance that isn't most of all the relevance of a living and recorded *relation*. It has ceased then to know itself in any degree as an estimate, has shaken off the anxieties of circumspection and comparison and just grown happy to act as an attachment pure and simple, an effect of life's own logic, but in the ashes of which the wonted fires of youth need but to be blown upon for betrayal of a glow. Reflective appreciation may have originally been concerned, whether at its most or at its least, but it is well over, to our infinite relief—yes, to our immortal comfort, I think; the interval back cannot again be bridged. We simply sit with our enjoyed gain, our residual rounded possession in our lap; a safe old treasure, which has ceased to shrink, if indeed also perhaps greatly to swell, and all that further touches it is the fine vibration set up if the name we know it all by is called into question—perhaps however little.

It was by George Eliot's name that I was to go on knowing, was never to cease to know, a great treasure of beauty and humanity, of applied and achieved art, a testimony, historic as well as æsthetic, to the deeper interest of the intricate English aspects; and I now allow the vibration, as I have called it, all its play—quite as if I had been wronged even by my own hesitation as to whether to pick up my anecdote. That scruple wholly fades with the sense of how I must at the very time have foreseen that here was one of those associations that would determine in the far future an exquisite inability to revise it. Middlemarch had not then appeared—we of the faith were still to enjoy that saturation, and Felix Holt the radical was upwards of three years old; the impetus proceeding from this work, however, was still fresh enough in my pulses to have quickened the palpitation of my finding myself in presence. I had rejoiced without reserve in Felix Holt—the illusion of reading which, outstretched on my then too frequently inevitable bed at Swampscott during a couple of very hot days of the summer of 1866, comes back to me, followed by that in sooth of sitting up again, at no great ease, to indite with all promptness a review of the delightful thing, the place of appearance of which nothing could now induce me to name, shameless about the general fact as I may have been at the hour itself: over such a feast of fine rich natural tone did I feel myself earnestly bend. Quite unforgettable to me the art and truth with which the note of this tone was struck in the beautiful prologue and the bygone appearances, a hundred of the outward and visible signs of the author's own young rural and midmost England, made to hold us by their harmony. The book was not, if I rightly remember, altogether genially greeted, but I was to hold fast to the charm I had thankfully suffered it, I had been conscious of absolutely needing it, to work.

Exquisite the remembrance of how it wouldn't have "done" for me at all, in relation to other inward matters, not to strain from the case the last drop of its happiest sense. And I had even with the cooling of the first glow so little gone back upon it, as we have nowadays learned to say, had in fact so gone forward, floated by its wave of superlative intended benignity, that, once in the cool quiet drawing-room at North Bank I knew myself steeped in still deeper depths of the medium. G. H. Lewes was absent for the time on an urgent errand; one of his sons, on a visit at the house, had been suddenly taken with a violent attack of pain, the heritage of a bad accident not long before in the West Indies, a suffered onset from an angry bull, I seem to recall, who had tossed or otherwise mauled him, and, though beaten off, left him considerably compromised—these facts being promptly imparted to us, in no small flutter, by our distinguished lady, who came in to us from another room, where she had been with the hapless young man while his father appealed to the nearest good chemist for some known specific. It infinitely moved me to see so great a celebrity quite humanly and familiarly agitated—even with something clear and noble in it too, to which, as well as to the extraordinarily interesting dignity of her whole odd personal conformation, I remember thinking her black silk dress and the lace mantilla attached to her head and keeping company on either side with the low-falling thickness of her dark hair effectively contributed. I have found myself, my life long, attaching value to every noted thing in respect to a great person—and George Eliot struck me on the spot as somehow *illustratively* great; never at any rate has the impression of those troubled moments faded from me, nor that at once of a certain high grace in her anxiety and a frank immediate appreciation of our presence, modest embarrassed folk as we were. It took me no long time to thrill with the sense, sublime in its unexpectedness, that we were perhaps, or indeed quite clearly, helping her to pass the time till Mr. Lewes's return—after which he would again post off for Mr. Paget the pre-eminent surgeon; and I see involved with this the perfect amenity of her assisting us, as it were, to assist her, through unrelinquished proper talk, due responsible remark and report, in the last degree suggestive to me, on a short holiday taken with Mr. Lewes in the south of France, whence they had just returned. Yes indeed, the lightest words of great persons are so little as any words of others are that I catch myself again inordinately struck with her dropping it off-hand that the mistral, scourge of their excursion, had blown them into Avignon, where they had gone, I think, to see J. S. Mill, only to blow them straight out again—the figure put it so before us; as well as with the moral interest, the absence of the *banal*, in their having, on the whole scene, found pleasure further poisoned by the frequency in all those parts of "evil faces: oh the evil faces!" *That* recorded source of suffering enormously affected me—I felt it as beautifully characteristic: I had never heard an *impression de voyage* so little tainted with the superficial or the vulgar. I was myself at the time in the thick of impressions, and it was true that they would have seemed to me rather to fail of life, of their own doubtless inferior kind, if submitting beyond a certain point to be touched with that sad or, as who should say, that grey colour: Mrs. Lewes's were, it appeared, predominantly so touched, and I could at once admire it in them and wonder if they didn't pay for this by some lack of intensity on other sides. Why I didn't more impute to her, or to them, that possible lack is more than I can say, since under the law of moral earnestness the vulgar and the trivial would be then involved in the poor observations of my own making—a conclusion sufficiently depressing.

However, I didn't find myself depressed, and I didn't find the great mind that was so good as to shine upon us at that awkward moment however dimly anything but augmented; what was its sensibility to the evil faces but part of the large old tenderness which the occasion had caused to overflow and on which we were presently floated back into the room she had left?—where we might perhaps beguile a little the impatience of the sufferer waiting for relief. We ventured in our flutter to doubt whether we *should* beguile, we held back with a certain delicacy from this irruption, and if there was a momentary wonderful and beautiful conflict I remember how our yielding struck me as crowned with the finest grace it could possibly have, that of the prodigious privilege of humouring, yes literally humouring so renowned a spirit at a moment when we could really match our judgment with hers. For the injured young man, in the other and the larger room, simply lay stretched on his back on the floor, the posture apparently least painful to him—though painful enough at the best I easily saw on kneeling beside him, after my first dismay, to ask if I could in any way ease him. I see his face again, fair and young and flushed, with its vague little smile and its moist brow; I recover the moment or two during which we sought to make natural conversation in his presence, and my question as to what conversation *was* natural; and then as his father's return still failed my having the inspiration that at once terminated the strain of the scene and yet prolonged the sublime connection. Mightn't *I* then hurry off for Mr. Paget?—on whom, as fast as a cab could carry me, I would wait with the request that he would come at the first possible moment to the rescue. Mrs. Lewes's and our stricken companion's instant appreciation of this offer lent me wings on which I again feel myself borne very much as if suddenly acting as a messenger of the gods—surely I had never come so near to performing in that character. I shook off my fellow visitor for swifter cleaving of the air, and I recall still feeling that I cleft it even in the dull four-wheeler of other days which, on getting out of the house, I recognised as the only object animating, at a distance, the long blank Sunday vista beside the walled-out Regent's Park. I crawled to Hanover Square—or was it Cavendish? I let the question stand—and, after learning at the great man's door that though he was not at home he was soon expected back and would receive my message without delay, cherished for the rest of the day the particular quality of my vibration.

It was doubtless even excessive in proportion to its cause—yet in what else but that consisted the force and the use of vibrations? It was by their excess that one knew them for such, as one for that matter only knew things in general worth knowing. I didn't know what I had expected as an effect of our offered homage, but I had somehow not, at the best, expected a relation—and now a relation had been dramatically determined. It would exist for me if I should never again in all the world ask a feather's weight of it; for myself, that is, it would simply never be able not somehow to act. Its virtue was not in truth at all flagrantly to be put to the proof—any opportunity for that underwent at the best a considerable lapse; but why wasn't it intensely acting, none the less, during the time when, before being in London again for any length of stay, I found it intimately concerned in my perusal of Middlemarch, so soon then to appear, and even in that of Deronda, its intervention on behalf of which defied any chill of time? And to these references I can but subjoin that they obviously most illustrate the operation of a sense for drama. The process of appropriation of the two fictions was experience, in great intensity, and roundabout the field was drawn the distinguishable ring of something that belonged equally to this condition and that embraced and further vivified the imaged mass, playing in upon it lights of surpassing fineness. So it was, at any rate, that my "relation"—for I didn't go so far as to call it "ours"—helped me to squeeze further values from the intrinsic substance of the copious final productions I have named, a weight of variety, dignity and beauty of which I have never allowed my measure to shrink.

Even this example of a rage for connections, I may also remark, doesn't deter me from the mention here, somewhat out of its order of time, of another of those in which my whole privilege of reference to Mrs. Lewes, such as it remained, was to look to be preserved. I stretch over the years a little to overtake it, and it calls up at once another person, the ornament, or at least the diversion, of a society long since extinct to me, but who, in common with every bearer of a name I yield to the temptation of writing, insists on profiting promptly by the fact of inscription—very much as if first tricking me into it and then proving it upon me. The extinct societies that once were so sure of themselves, how can they *not* stir again if the right touch, that of a hand they actually knew, however little they may have happened to heed it, reaches tenderly back to them? The touch *is* the retrieval, so far as it goes, setting up as it does heaven knows what undefeated continuity. I must have been present among the faithful at North Bank during a Sunday afternoon or two of the winter of '77 and '78—I was to see the great lady alone but on a single occasion before her death; but those attestations are all but lost to me now in the livelier pitch of a scene, as I can only call it, of which I feel myself again, all amusedly, rather as sacrificed witness. I had driven over with Mrs. Greville from Milford Cottage, in Surrey, to the villa George Eliot and George Lewes had not long before built themselves, and which they much inhabited, at Witley—this indeed, I well remember, in no great flush of assurance that my own measure of our intended felicity would be quite that of my buoyant hostess. But here exactly comes, with my memory of Mrs. Greville, from which numberless by-memories dangle, the interesting question that makes for my recall why things happened, under her much-waved wing, not in any too coherent fashion—and this even though it was never once given her, I surmise, to guess that they anywhere fell short. So gently used, all round indeed, was this large, elegant, extremely near-sighted and extremely demonstrative lady, whose genius was all for friendship, admiration, declamation and expenditure, that one doubted whether in the whole course of her career she had ever once been brought up, as it were, against a recognised reality; other at least perhaps than the tiresome cost of the materially agreeable in life and the perverse appearance, at times, that though she "said" things, otherwise recited choice morceaux, whether French or English, with a marked oddity of manner, of "attack," a general incongruity of drawing-room art, the various contributive elements, hour, scene, persuaded patience and hushed attention, were perforce a precarious quantity.

It is in that bygone old grace of the unexploded factitious, the air of a thousand dimmed illusions and more or less early Victorian beatitudes on the part of the blandly idle and the supposedly accomplished, that Mrs. Greville, with her exquisite good-nature and her innocent fatuity, is embalmed for me; so that she becomes in that light a truly shining specimen, almost the image or compendium of a whole side of a social order. Just so she has happy suggestion; just so, whether or no by a twist of my mind toward the enviability of certain complacencies of faith and taste that we would yet neither live back into if we could, nor can catch again if we would. I see my forgotten friend of that moist autumn afternoon of our call, and of another, on the morrow, which I shall not pass over, as having rustled and gushed and protested and performed through her term under a kind of protection by the easy-going gods that is not of this fierce age. Amiabilities and absurdities, harmless serenities and vanities, pretensions and undertakings unashamed, still profited by the mildness of the critical air and the benignity of the social—on the right side at least of the social line. It had struck me from the first that nowhere so much as in England was it fortunate to *be* fortunate, and that against that condition, once it had somehow been handed down and determined, a number of the sharp truths that one might privately apprehend beat themselves beautifully in vain. I say beautifully for I confess without scruple to have found again and again at that time an attaching charm in the general exhibition of enjoyed immunity, paid for as it was almost always by the personal amenity, the practice of all sorts of pleasantness; if it kept the gods themselves for the time in good-humour, one was willing enough, or at least I was, to be on the side of the gods. Unmistakable too, as I seem to recover it, was the positive interest of watching and noting, roundabout one, for the turn, or rather for the blest continuity, of their benevolence: such an appeal proceeded, in this, that and the other particular case, from the fool's paradise really rounded and preserved, before one's eyes, for those who were so good as to animate it. There was always the question of how long they would be left to, and the growth of one's fine suspense, not to say one's frank little gratitude, as the miracle repeated itself.

All of which, I admit, dresses in many reflections the small circumstance that Milford Cottage, with its innumerable red candles and candle-shades, had affected me as the most embowered retreat for social innocence that it was possible to conceive, and as absolutely settling the question of whether the practice of pleasantness mightn't quite ideally pay for the fantastic protectedness. The red candles in the red shades have remained with me, inexplicably, as a vivid note of this pitch, shedding their rosy light, with the autumn gale, the averted reality, all shut out, upon such felicities of feminine helplessness as I couldn't have prefigured in advance and as exemplified, for further gathering in, the possibilities of the old tone. Nowhere had the evening curtains seemed so drawn, nowhere the copious service so soft, nowhere the second volume of the new novel, "half-uncut," so close to one's hand, nowhere the exquisite head and incomparable brush of the domesticated collie such an attestation of *that* standard at least, nowhere the harmonies of accident—of intention was more than one could say—so incapable of a wrong deflection. That society would lack the highest finish without some such distributed clusters of the thoroughly gentle, the mildly presumptuous and the inveterately mistaken, was brought home to me there, in fine, to a tune with which I had no quarrel, perverse enough as I had been from an early time to know but the impulse to egg on society to the fullest discharge of any material stirring within its breast and not making for cruelty or brutality, mere baseness or mere stupidity, that would fall into a picture or a scene. The quality of serene anxiety on the part for instance of exquisite Mrs. Thellusson, Mrs. Greville's mother, was by itself a plea for any privilege one should fancy her perched upon; and I scarce know if this be more or be less true because the anxiety—at least as I culled its fragrance—was all about the most secondary and superfluous small matters alone. It struck me, I remember, as a new and unexpected form of the pathetic altogether; and there was no form of the pathetic, any more than of the tragic or the comic, that didn't serve as another pearl for one's lengthening string. And I pass over what was doubtless the happiest stroke in the composition, the fact of its involving, as all-distinguished husband of the other daughter, an illustrious soldier and servant of his sovereign, of his sovereigns that were successively to be, than against whose patient handsome bearded presence the whole complexus of femininities and futilities couldn't have been left in more tolerated and more contrasted relief; pass it over to remind myself of how, in my particular friend of the three, the comic and the tragic were presented in a confusion that made the least intended of them at any moment take effectively the place of the most. The impression, that is, was never that of the sentiment operating—save indeed perhaps when the dear lady applied her faculty for frank imitation of the ridiculous, which she then quite directly and remarkably achieved; but that she could be comic, that she *was* comic, was what least appeased her unrest, and there were reasons enough, in a word, why her failure of the grand manner or the penetrating note should evoke the idea of their opposites perfectly achieved. She sat, alike in adoration and emulation, at the feet of my admirable old friend Fanny Kemble, the good-nature of whose consent to "hear" her was equalled only by the immediately consequent action of the splendidly corrective spring on the part of that unsurpassed subject of the dramatic afflatus fairly, or, as I should perhaps above all say, contradictiously provoked. Then aspirant and auditor, rash adventurer and shy alarmist, were swept away together in the gust of magnificent rightness and beauty, no scrap of the far-scattered prime proposal being left to pick up.

Which detail of reminiscence has again stayed my course to the Witley Villa, when even on the way I quaked a little with my sense of what *generally* most awaited or overtook my companion's prime proposals. What had come most to characterise the Leweses to my apprehension was that there couldn't be a thing in the world about which they weren't, and on the most conceded and assured grounds, almost scientifically particular; which presumption, however, only added to the relevance of one's learning how such a matter as their relation with Mrs. Greville could in accordance with noble consistencies be carried on. I could trust *her* for it perfectly, as she knew no law but that of innocent and exquisite aberration, never wanting and never less than consecrating, and I fear I but took refuge for the rest in declining all responsibility. I remember trying to say to myself that, even such as we were, our visit couldn't but scatter a little the weight of cloud on the Olympus we scaled—given the dreadful drenching afternoon we were after all an imaginable short solace there; and this indeed would have borne me through to the end save for an incident which, with a quite ideal logic, left our adventure an approved ruin. I see again our bland, benign, commiserating hostess beside the fire in a chill desert of a room where the master of the house guarded the opposite hearthstone, and I catch once more the impression of no occurrence of anything at all appreciable but their liking us to have come, with our terribly trivial contribution, mainly from a prevision of how they should more devoutly like it when we departed. It is remarkable, but the occasion yields me no single echo of a remark on the part of any of us—nothing more than the sense that our great author herself peculiarly suffered from the fury of the elements, and that they had about them rather the minimum of the paraphernalia of reading and writing, not to speak of that of tea, a conceivable feature of the hour, but which was not provided for. Again I felt touched with privilege, but not, as in '69, with a form of it redeemed from barrenness by a motion of my own, and the taste of barrenness was in fact in my mouth under the effect of our taking leave. We did so with considerable flourish till we had passed out to the hall again, indeed to the door of the waiting carriage, toward which G. H. Lewes himself all sociably, *then* above all conversingly, wafted us—yet staying me by a sudden remembrance before I had entered the brougham and signing me to wait while he repaired his omission. I returned to the doorstep, whence I still see him reissue from the room we had just left and hurry toward me across the hall shaking high the pair of blue-bound volumes his allusion to the uninvited, the verily importunate loan of which by Mrs. Greville had lingered on the air after his dash in quest of them; "Ah those books—take them away, please, away, away!" I hear him unreservedly plead while he thrusts them again at me, and I scurry back into our conveyance, where, and where only, settled afresh with my companion,

I venture to assure myself of the horrid truth that had squinted at me as I relieved our good friend of his superfluity. What indeed was this superfluity but the two volumes of my own precious "last"—we were still in the blest age of volumes—presented by its author to the lady of Milford Cottage, and by her, misguided votary, dropped with the best conscience in the world into the Witley abyss, out of which it had jumped with violence, under the touch of accident, straight up again into my own exposed face?

The bruise inflicted there I remember feeling for the moment only as sharp, such a mixture of delightful small questions at once salved it over and such a charm in particular for me to my recognising that this particular wrong—inflicted all unawares, which exactly made it sublime—was the only rightness of our visit. Our hosts hadn't so much as connected book with author, or author with visitor, or visitor with anything but the convenience of his ridding them of an unconsidered trifle; grudging as they so justifiedly did the impingement of such matters on their consciousness. The vivid demonstration of one's failure to penetrate there had been in the sweep of Lewes's gesture, which could scarce have been bettered by his actually wielding a broom. I think nothing passed between us in the brougham on revelation of the identity of the offered treat so emphatically declined—I see that I couldn't have laughed at it to the confusion of my gentle neighbour. But I quite recall my grasp of the *interest* of our distinguished friends' inaccessibility to the unattended plea, with the light it seemed to throw on what it was really to *be* attended. Never, never save as attended—by presumptions, that is, far other than any then hanging about one—would one so much as desire *not* to be pushed out of sight. I needn't attempt, however, to supply all the links in the chain of association which led to my finally just qualified beatitude: I had been served right enough in all conscience, but the pity was that Mrs. Greville had been. This I never wanted for her; and I may add, in the connection, that I discover now no grain of false humility in my having enjoyed in my own person adorning such a tale. There was positively a fine high thrill in thinking of persons—or at least of a person, for any fact about Lewes was but derivative—engaged in my own pursuit and yet detached, by what I conceived, detached by a pitch of intellectual life, from all that made it actual to myself. *There* was the lift of contemplation, there the inspiring image and the big supporting truth; the pitch of intellectual life in the very fact of which we seemed, my hostess and I, to have caught our celebrities sitting in that queer bleak way wouldn't have bullied me in the least if it hadn't been the centre of such a circle of gorgeous creation. It was the fashion among the profane in short either to misdoubt, before George Eliot's canvas, the latter's backing of rich thought, or else to hold that this matter of philosophy, and even if but of the philosophic vocabulary, thrust itself through to the confounding of the picture. But with that thin criticism I wasn't, as I have already intimated, to have a moment's patience; I was to become, I was to remain—I take pleasure in repeating—even a very Derondist of Derondists, for my own wanton joy: which amounts to saying that I found the figured, coloured tapestry *always* vivid enough to brave no matter what complication of the stitch.

VI

I take courage to confess moreover that I am carried further still by the current on which Mrs. Greville, friend of the super-eminent, happens to have launched me; for I can neither forbear a glance at one or two of the other adventures promoted by her, nor in the least dissociate her from that long aftertaste of them, such as they were, which I have positively cultivated. I ask myself first, however, whether or no our drive to Aldworth, on the noble height of Blackdown, had been preceded by the couple of occasions in London on which I was to feel I saw the Laureate most at his ease, yet on reflection concluding that the first of these—and the fewest days must have separated them—formed my prime introduction to the poet I had earliest known and best loved. The revelational evening I speak of is peopled, to my memory, not a little, yet with a confusedness out of which Tennyson's own presence doesn't at all distinctly emerge; he was occupying a house in Eaton Place, as appeared then his wont, for the earlier weeks of the spring, and I seem to recover that I had "gone on" to it, after dining somewhere else, under protection of my supremely kind old friend the late Lord Houghton, to whom I was indebted in those years for a most promiscuous befriending. He must have been of the party, and Mrs. Greville quite independently must, since I catch again the vision of her, so expansively and voluminously seated that she might fairly have been couchant, so to say, for the proposed characteristic act—there was a deliberation about it that precluded the idea of a spring; that, namely, of addressing something of the Laureate's very own to the Laureate's very face. Beyond the sense that he took these things with a gruff philosophy—and could always repay them, on the spot, in heavily-shovelled coin of the same mint, since it *was* a question of his genius—I gather in again no determined impression, unless it may have been, as could only be probable, the effect of fond prefigurements utterly blighted.

The fond prefigurements of youthful piety are predestined more often than not, I think, experience interfering, to strange and violent shocks; from which no general appeal is conceivable save by the prompt preclusion either of faith or of knowledge, a sad choice at the best. No other such illustration recurs to me of the possible refusal of those two conditions of an acquaintance to recognise each other at a given hour as the silent crash of which I was to be conscious several years later, in Paris, when placed in presence of M. Ernest Renan, from the surpassing distinction of whose literary face, with its exquisite finish of every feature, I had from far back extracted every sort of shining gage, a presumption general and positive. Widely enough to sink all interest—that was the dreadful thing—opened there the chasm between the implied, as I had taken it, and the attested, as I had, at the first blush, to take it; so that one was in fact scarce to know what might have happened if interest hadn't by good fortune already reached such a compass as to stick half way down the descent. What interest *can* survive becomes thus, surely, as much one of the lessons of life as the number of ways in which it remains impossible. What comes up in face of the shocks, as I have called them, is the question of a shift of every supposition, a change of base under fire, as it were; which must take place successfully if one's advance be not abandoned altogether. I remember that I saw the Tennyson directly presented as just utterly other than the Tennyson indirectly, and if the readjustment, for acquaintance, was less difficult than it was to prove in the case of the realised Renan the obligation to accept the difference—wholly as difference and without reference to strict loss or gain—was like a rap on the knuckles of a sweet superstition. Fine, fine, fine could he only be—fine in the sense of that quality in the texture of his verse, which had appealed all along by its most inward principle to one's taste, and had by the same stroke shown with what a force of lyric energy and sincerity the kind of beauty so engaged for could be associated. Was it that I had preconceived him in that light as pale and penetrating, as emphasising in every aspect the fact that he was fastidious? was it that I had supposed him more fastidious than really *could* have been— at the best for that effect? was it that the grace of the man *couldn't*, by my measure, but march somehow with the grace of the poet, given a perfection of this grace? was it in fine that style of a particular kind, when so highly developed, seemed logically to leave no room for other quite contradictious kinds? These were considerations of which I recall the pressure, at the same time that I fear I have no account of them to give after they have fairly faced the full, the monstrous demonstration that Tennyson was not Tennysonian. The desperate sequel to that was that he thereby changed one's own state too, one's beguiled, one's æsthetic; for what *could* this strange apprehension do but reduce the Tennysonian amount altogether? It dried up, to a certain extent, that is, in my own vessel of sympathy—leaving me so to ask whether it was before or after that I should take myself for the bigger fool. There had been folly somewhere; yet let me add that once I recognised this, once I felt the old fond pitch drop of itself, not alone inevitably, but very soon quite conveniently and while I magnanimously granted that the error had been mine and nobody's else at all, an odd prosaic pleasantness set itself straight up, substitutionally, over the whole ground, which it swept clear of every single premeditated effect. It made one's perceptive condition purely profane, reduced it somehow to having rather the excess of awkwardness than the excess of felicity to reckon with; yet still again, as I say, enabled a compromise to work.

The compromise in fact worked beautifully under my renewal of impression—for which a second visit at Eaton Place offered occasion; and this even though I had to interweave with the scene as best I might a highly complicating influence. To speak of James Russell Lowell's influence as above all complicating on any scene to the interest of which he contributed may superficially seem a perverse appreciation of it; and yet in the light of that truth only do I recover the full sense of his value, his interest, the moving moral of his London adventure—to find myself already bumping so straight against which gives me, I confess, a sufficiently portentous shake. He comes in, as it were, by a force not to be denied, as soon as I look at him again—as soon as I find him for instance on the doorstep in Eaton Place at the hour of my too approaching it for luncheon as he had just done. There he is, with the whole question of him, at once before me, and literally superimposed by that fact on any minor essence. I quake, positively, with the apprehension of the commemorative dance he may lead me; but for the moment, just here, I steady myself with an effort and go in with him to his having the Laureate's personal acquaintance, by every symptom, and rather to my surprise, all to make. Mrs. Tennyson's luncheon table was an open feast, with places for possible when not assured guests; and no one but the American Minister, scarce more than just installed, and his extremely attached compatriot sat down at first with our gracious hostess. The board considerably stretched, and after it had been indicated to Lowell that he had best sit at the end near the window, where the Bard would presently join him, I remained, near our hostess, separated from him for some little time by an unpeopled waste. Hallam came in all genially and auspiciously, yet only to brush us with his blessing and say he was lunching elsewhere, and my wonder meanwhile hung about the representative of my country, who, though partaking of offered food, appeared doomed to disconnection from us. I may say at once that my wonder was always unable *not* to hang about this admired and cherished friend when other persons, especially of the eminent order, were concerned in the scene. The case was quite other for the unshared relation, or when it was shared by one or other of three or four of our common friends who had the gift of determining happily the pitch of ease; suspense, not to say anxiety, as to the possible turn or drift of the affair quite dropped—I rested then, we alike rested, I ever felt, in a golden confidence. This last was so definitely not the note of my attention to him, so far as I might indulge it, in the wider social world, that I shall not scruple, occasion offering, to inquire into the reasons of the difference. For I can only see the ghosts of my friends, by this token, as "my" J. R. L. and whoever; which means that my imagination, of the wanton life of which these remarks pretend but to form the record, had appropriated them, under the prime contact—from the moment the prime contact had successfully worked—once for all, and contributed the light in which they were constantly exposed.

Yes, delightful I shall undertake finding it, and perhaps even making it, to read J. R. L.'s exposure back into *its* light; which I in fact see begin to shine for me more amply during those very minutes of our wait for our distinguished host and even the several that followed the latter's arrival and his seating himself opposite the unknown guest, whose identity he had failed to grasp. Nothing, exactly, could have made dear Lowell more "my" Lowell, as I have presumed to figure him, than the stretch of uncertainty so supervening and which, in its form of silence at first completely unbroken between the two poets, rapidly took on for me monstrous proportions. I conversed with my gentle neighbour during what seemed an eternity—really but hearing, as the minutes sped, all that Tennyson didn't say to Lowell and all that Lowell wouldn't on any such compulsion as that say to Tennyson. I like, however, to hang again upon the hush—for the sweetness of the relief of its break by the fine Tennysonian growl. I had never dreamed, no, of a growling Tennyson—I had too utterly otherwise fantasticated; but no line of Locksley Hall rolled out as I was to happen soon after to hear it, could have been sweeter than the interrogative sound of "Do you know anything about *Lowell*?" launched on the chance across the table and crowned at once by Mrs. Tennyson's anxious quaver: "Why, my dear, this *is* Mr. Lowell!" The clearance took place successfully enough, and the incident, I am quite aware, seems to shrink with it; in spite of which I still cherish the reduced reminiscence for its connections: so far as my vision of Lowell was concerned they began at that moment so to multiply. A belated guest or two more came in, and I wish I could for my modesty's sake refer to this circumstance alone the fact that nothing more of the occasion survives for me save the intense but restricted glow of certain instants, in another room, to which we had adjourned for smoking and where my alarmed sense of the Bard's restriction to giving what he had as a bard only became under a single turn of his hand a vision of quite general munificence. Incredibly, inconceivably, he had *read*—and not only read but admired, and not only admired but understandingly referred; referred, time and some accident aiding, the appreciated object, a short tale I had lately put forth, to its actually present author, who could scarce believe his ears on hearing the thing superlatively commended; pronounced, that is, by the illustrious speaker, more to his taste than no matter what other like attempt. Nothing would induce me to disclose the title of the piece, which has little to do with the matter; my point is but in its having on the spot been matter of pure romance to me that I was there and positively so addressed. For it was a solution, the happiest in the world, and from which I at once extracted enormities of pleasure: my relation to whatever had bewildered me simply became perfect: the author of In Memoriam had "liked" my own twenty pages, and his doing so was a gage of his grace in which I felt I should rest forever—in which I have in fact rested to this hour. My own basis of liking—such a blessed supersession of all worryings and wonderings!—was accordingly established, and has met every demand made of it.

Greatest was to have been, I dare say, the demand to which I felt it exposed by the drive over to Aldworth with Mrs. Greville which I noted above and which took place, if I am not mistaken, on the morrow of our drive to Witley. A different shade of confidence and comfort, I make out, accompanied this experiment: I believed more, for reasons I shall not now attempt to recover, in the furthermost maintenance of our flying bridge, the final piers of which, it was indubitable, *had* at Witley given way. What could have been moreover less like G. H. Lewes's valedictory hurl back upon us of the printed appeal in which I was primarily concerned than that so recent and so directly opposed passage of the Eaton Place smoking-room, thanks to which I could nurse a certified security all along the road? I surrendered to security, I perhaps even grossly took my ease in it; and I was to breathe from beginning to end of our visit, which began with our sitting again at luncheon, an air—so unlike that of Witley!—in which it seemed to me frankly that nothing but the blest obvious, or at least the blest outright, could so much as attempt to live. These elements hung sociably and all auspiciously about us—it was a large and simple and almost empty occasion; yet empty without embarrassment, rather as from a certain high guardedness or defensiveness of situation, literally indeed from the material, the local sublimity, the fact of our all upliftedly hanging together over one of the grandest sweeps of view in England. Remembered passages again people, however, in their proportion, the excess of opportunity; each with that conclusive note of the outright all unadorned. What could have partaken more of this quality for instance than the question I was startled to hear launched before we had left the table by the chance of Mrs. Greville's having happened to mention in some connection one of her French relatives, Mademoiselle Laure de Sade? It had fallen on my own ear—the mention at least had—with a certain effect of unconscious provocation; but this was as nothing to its effect on the ear of our host. "De Sade?" he at once exclaimed with interest—and with the consequence, I may frankly add, of my wondering almost to ecstasy, that is to the ecstasy of curiosity, to what length he would proceed. He proceeded admirably—admirably for the triumph of simplification—to the very greatest length imaginable, as was signally promoted by the fact that clearly no one present, with a single exception, recognised the name or the nature of the scandalous, the long ignored, the at last all but unnameable author; least of all the gentle relative of Mademoiselle Laure, who listened with the blankest grace to her friend's enumeration of his titles to infamy, among which that of his most notorious work was pronounced. It was the homeliest, frankest, most domestic passage, as who should say, and most remarkable for leaving none of us save myself, by my impression, in the least embarrassed or bewildered; largely, I think, because of the failure—a failure the most charmingly flat— of all measure on the part of auditors and speaker alike of what might be intended or understood, of what, in fine, the latter was talking about.

He struck me in truth as neither knowing nor communicating knowledge, and I recall how I felt this note in his own case to belong to that general intimation with which the whole air was charged of the want of proportion between the great spaces and reaches and echoes commanded, the great eminence attained, and the quantity and variety of experience supposable. So to discriminate was in a manner to put one's hand on the key, and thereby to find one's self in presence of a rare and anomalous, but still scarcely the less beautiful fact. The assured and achieved conditions, the serenity, the security, the success, to put it vulgarly, shone in the light of their easiest law—that by which they emerge early from the complication of life, the great adventure of sensibility, and find themselves determined once for all, fortunately fixed, all consecrated and consecrating. If I should speak of this impression as that of glory without history, that of the poetic character more worn than paid for, or at least more saved than spent, I should doubtless much over-emphasise; but such, or something like it, was none the less the explanation that met one's own fond fancy of the scene after one had cast about for it. For I allow myself thus to repeat that I was so moved to cast about, and perhaps at no moment more than during the friendly analysis of the reputation of M. de Sade. Was I not present at some undreamed-of demonstration of the absence of the remoter real, the real other than immediate and exquisite, other than guaranteed and enclosed, in landscape, friendship, fame, above all in consciousness of awaited and admired and self-consistent inspiration?

The question was indeed to be effectively answered for me, and everything meanwhile continued to play into this prevision—even to the pleasant growling note heard behind me, as the Bard followed with Mrs. Greville, who had permitted herself apparently some mild extravagance of homage: "Oh yes, you may do what you like—so long as you don't kiss me before the cabman!" The allusion was explained for us, if I remember—a matter of some more or less recent leave-taking of admirer and admired in London on his putting her down at her door after being taken to the play or wherever; between the rugged humour of which reference and the other just commemorated there wasn't a pin to choose, it struck me, for a certain old-time Lincolnshire ease or comfortable stay-at-home license. But it was later on, when, my introductress having accompanied us, I sat upstairs with him in his study, that he might read to us some poem of his own that we should venture to propose, it was then that mystifications dropped, that everything in the least dislocated fell into its place, and that image and picture stamped themselves strongly and finally, or to the point even, as I recover it, of leaving me almost too little to wonder about. He had not got a third of the way through Locksley Hall, which, my choice given me, I had made bold to suggest he should spout—for I had already heard him spout in Eaton Place—before I had begun to wonder that I didn't wonder, didn't at least wonder more consumedly; as a very little while back I should have made sure of my doing on any such prodigious occasion. I sat at one of the windows that hung over space, noting how the windy, watery autumn day, sometimes sheeting it all with rain, called up the dreary, dreary moorland or the long dun wolds; I pinched myself for the determination of my identity and hung on the reader's deep-voiced chant for the credibility of his: I asked myself in fine why, in complete deviation from everything that would have seemed from far back certain for the case, I failed to swoon away under the heaviest pressure I had doubtless ever known the romantic situation bring to bear. So lucidly all the while I considered, so detachedly I judged, so dissentingly, to tell the whole truth, I listened; pinching myself, as I say, not at all to keep from swooning, but much rather to set up some rush of sensibility. It was all interesting, it was at least all odd; but why in the name of poetic justice had one anciently heaved and flushed with one's own recital of the splendid stuff if one was now only to sigh in secret "Oh dear, oh dear"? The author lowered the whole pitch, that of expression, that of interpretation above all; I heard him, in cool surprise, take even more out of his verse than he had put in, and so bring me back to the point I had immediately and privately made, the point that he wasn't Tennysonian. I felt him as he went on and on lose that character beyond repair, and no effect of the organ-roll, of monotonous majesty, no suggestion of the long echo, availed at all to save it. What the case came to for me, I take it—and by the case I mean the intellectual, the artistic— was that it lacked the intelligence, the play of discrimination, I should have taken for granted in it, and thereby, brooding monster that I was, born to discriminate *à tout propos*, lacked the interest.

Detached I have mentioned that I had become, and it was doubtless at such a rate high time for that; though I hasten to repeat that with the close of the incident I was happily able to feel a new sense in the whole connection established. My critical reaction hadn't in the least invalidated our great man's being a Bard—it had in fact made him and left him more a Bard than ever: it had only settled to my perception as not before what a Bard might and mightn't be. The character was just a rigid idiosyncrasy, to which everything in the man conformed, but which supplied nothing outside of itself, and which above all was not intellectually wasteful or heterogeneous, conscious as it could only be of its intrinsic breadth and weight. On two or three occasions of the aftertime I was to hear Browning read out certain of his finest pages, and this exactly with all the exhibition of point and authority, the expressive particularisation, so to speak, that I had missed on the part of the Laureate; an observation through which the author of Men and Women appeared, in spite of the beauty and force of his demonstration, as little as possible a Bard. He particularised if ever a man did, was heterogeneous and profane, composed of pieces and patches that betrayed some creak of joints, and addicted to the excursions from which these were brought home; so that he had to *prove* himself a poet, almost against all presumptions, and with all the assurance and all the character he could use. Was not this last in especial, the character, so close to the surface, with which Browning fairly bristled, what was most to come out in his personal delivery of the fruit of his genius? It came out almost to harshness; but the result was that what he read showed extraordinary life. During that audition at Aldworth the question seemed on the contrary not of life at all—save, that is, of one's own; which was exactly not the question. With all the resonance of the chant, the whole thing was yet *still*, with all the long swing of its motion it yet remained where it was—heaving doubtless grandly enough up and down and beautiful to watch as through the superposed veils of its long self-consciousness. By all of which I don't mean to say that I was not, on the day at Aldworth, thoroughly reconciled to learning what a Bard consisted of; for that came as soon as I had swallowed my own mistake—the mistake of having supposed Tennyson something subtly other than one. I had supposed, probably, such an impossibility, had, to repeat my term, so absurdly fantasticated, that the long journey round and about the truth no more than served me right; just as after all it at last left me quite content.

VII

It left me moreover, I become aware—or at least it now leaves me—fingering the loose ends of this particular free stretch of my tapestry; so that, with my perhaps even extravagant aversion to loose ends, I can but try for a moment to interweave them. There dangles again for me least confusedly, I think, the vision of a dinner at Mrs. Greville's—and I like even to remember that Cadogan Place, where memories hang thick for me, was the scene of it—which took its light from the presence of Louisa Lady Waterford, who took hers in turn from that combination of rare beauty with rare talent which the previous Victorian age had for many years not ceased to acclaim. It insists on coming back to me with the utmost vividness that Lady Waterford was illustrational, historically, preciously so, meeting one's largest demand for the blest recovery, when possible, of some glimmer of the sense of personal beauty, to say nothing of personal "accomplishment," as our fathers were appointed to enjoy it. Scarce to be sated that form of wonder, to my own imagination, I confess—so that I fairly believe there was no moment at which I wouldn't have been ready to turn my back for the time even on the most triumphant actuality of form and feature if a chance apprehension of a like force as it played on the sensibility of the past had competed. And this for a reason I fear I can scarce explain—unless, when I come to consider it, by the perversity of a conviction that the conditions of beauty have improved, though those of character, in the fine old sense, may not, and that with these the measure of it is more just, the appreciation, as who should say, more competent and the effect more completely attained.

What the question seems thus to come to would be a consuming curiosity as to any cited old case of the spell in the very interest of one's catching it comparatively "out"; in the interest positively of the likelihood of one's doing so, and this in the face of so many great testifying portraits. My private perversity, as I here glance at it, has had its difficulties—most of all possibly that of one's addiction, in growing older, to allowing a supreme force to one's earlier, even one's earliest, estimates of physical felicity; or in other words that of the felt impulse to leave the palm for good looks to those who have reached out to it through the medium of our own history. If the conditions *grow* better for them why then should we have almost the habit of thinking better of our handsome folk dead than of our living?—and even to the very point of not resenting on the part of others similarly affected the wail of wonder as to what has strangely "become" of the happy types *d'antan*. I dodge that inquiry just now—we may meet it again; noting simply the fact that "old" pretenders to the particular crown I speak of—and in the sense especially of the pretension made rather for than by them—offered to my eyes a greater interest than the new, whom I was ready enough to take for granted, as one for the most part easily could; belonging as it exactly did on the other hand to the interest of their elders that *this* couldn't be so taken. That was just the attraction of the latter claim—that the grounds of it had to be made out, puzzled out verily on occasion, but that when they were recognised they had a force all their own. One would have liked to be able to clear the distinction between the new and the old of all ambiguity—explain, that is, how little the superficially invidious term was sometimes noted as having in common with the elderly: so much was it a clear light held up to the question that truly beautiful persons might be old without being elderly. Their juniors couldn't be new, unfortunately, without being youthful—unfortunately because the fact of youth, so far from dispelling ambiguity, positively introduced it. One made up one's mind thus that the only sure specimens were, and had to be, those acquainted with time, and with whom time, on its side, was acquainted; those in fine who had borne the test and still looked at it face to face. These were of one's own period of course—one looked at *them* face to, face; one blessedly hadn't to consider them by hearsay or to refer to any portrait of them for proof: indeed in presence of the resisting, the gained, cases one found one's self practically averse to old facts or old traditions of portraiture, accompanied by no matter what names.

All of which leads by an avenue I trust not unduly majestic up to that hour of contemplation during which I could see quite enough for the major interest what was meant by Lady Waterford's great reputation. Nothing could in fact have been more informing than so to see what was meant, than so copiously to share with admirers who had had their vision and passed on;

for if I spoke above of her image as illustrational this is because it affected me on the spot as so diffusing information. My impression was of course but the old story—to which my reader will feel himself treated, I fear, to satiety: when once I had drawn the curtain for the light shed by this or that or the other personal presence upon the society more or less intimately concerned in producing it the last thing I could think of was to darken the scene again. For this right or this wrong reason then Mrs. Greville's admirable guest struck me as flooding it; indebted in the highest degree to every art by which a commended appearance may have formed the habit of still suggesting commendation, she certainly—to my imagination at least—triumphed over time in the sense that if the years, in their generosity, went on helping her to live, her grace returned the favour by paying life back to them. I mean that she reanimated for the fond analyst the age in which persons of her type could so greatly flourish—it being ever so pertinently of her type, or at least of that of the age, that she was regarded as having cast the spell of genius as well as of beauty. She painted, and on the largest scale, with all confidence and facility, and nothing could have contributed more, by my sense, to what I glance at again as her illustrational value than the apparently widespread appreciation of this fact—taken together, that is, with one's own impression of the work of her hand. There it was that, like Mrs. Greville herself, yet in a still higher degree, she bore witness to the fine old felicity of the fortunate and the "great" under the "old" order which would have made it so good then to live could one but have been in their shoes. She determined in me, I remember, a renewed perception of the old order, a renewed insistence on one's having come just in time to see it begin to stretch back: a little earlier one wouldn't have had the light for this perhaps, and a little later it would have receded too much.

The precious persons, the surviving figures, who held up, as I may call it, the light were still here and there to be met; my sense being that the last of them, at least for any vision of mine, has now quite gone and that illustration—not to let that term slip—accordingly fails. We all now illustrate together, in higgledy-piggledy fashion, or as a vast monotonous mob, our own wonderful period and order, and nothing else; whereby the historic imagination, under its acuter need of facing backward, gropes before it with a vain gesture, missing, or all but missing, the concrete *other*, always other, specimen which has volumes to give where hearsay has only snippets. The old, as we call it, I recognise, doesn't disappear all at once; the *ancien régime* of our commonest reference survived the Revolution of our most horrific in patches and scraps, and I bring myself to say that even at my present writing I am aware of more than one individual on the scene about me touched *comparatively* with the elder grace. (I think of the difference between these persons and so nearly all other persons as a grace for reasons that become perfectly clear in the immediate presence of the former, but of which a generalising account is difficult.) None the less it used to be one of the finest of pleasures to acclaim and cherish, in case of meeting them, one and another of the *complete* examples of the conditions irrecoverable, even if, as I have already noted, they were themselves least intelligently conscious of these; and for the enjoyment of that critical emotion to draw one's own wanton line between the past and the present. The happy effect of such apparitions as Lady Waterford, to whom I thus undisseverably cling, though I might give her after all much like company, was that they made one draw it just where they might most profit from it. They profited in that they recruited my group of the fatuously fortunate, the class, as I seemed to see it, that had had the longest and happiest innings in history—happier and longer, on the whole, even than their congeners of the old French time—and for whom the future wasn't going to be, by most signs, anything like as bland and benedictory as the past. They placed *themselves* in the right perspective for appreciation, and did it quite without knowing, which was half the interest; did it simply by showing themselves with all the right grace and the right assurance. It was as if they had come up to the very edge of the ground that was going to begin to fail them; yet looking over it, looking on and on always, with a confidence still unalarmed. One would have turned away certainly from the sight of any actual catastrophe, wouldn't have watched the ground nearly fail, in a particular case, without a sense of gross indelicacy. I can scarcely say how vivid I felt the drama so preparing might become—that of the lapse of immemorial protection, that of the finally complete exposure of the immemorially protected. It might take place rather more intensely before the footlights of one's inner vision than on the trodden stage of Cadogan Place or wherever, but it corresponded none the less to realities all the while in course of enactment and which only wanted the attentive enough spectator. Nothing should I evermore see comparable to the large fond consensus of admiration enjoyed by my beatific fellow-guest's imputed command of the very palette of the Venetian and other masters—Titian's, Bonifazio's, Rubens's, where did the delightful agreement on the subject stop? and never again should a noble lady be lifted so still further aloft on the ecstatic breath of connoisseurship.

This last consciousness, confirming my impression of a climax that could only decline, didn't break upon me all at once but spread itself through a couple of subsequent occasions into which my remembrance of the dinner at Mrs. Greville's was richly to play. The first of these was a visit to an exhibition of Lady Waterford's paintings held, in Carlton House Terrace, under the roof of a friend of the artist, and, as it enriched the hour also to be able to feel, a friend, one of the most generously gracious, of my own; during which the reflection that "they" had indeed had their innings, and were still splendidly using for the purpose the very fag-end of the waning time, mixed itself for me with all the "wonderful colour" framed and arrayed, that blazed from the walls of the kindly great room, lent for the advantage of a charity, and lost itself in the general chorus of immense comparison and tender consecration. Later on a few days spent at a house of the greatest beauty and interest in Northumberland did wonders to round off my view; the place, occupied for the time by genial tenants, belonged to the family of Lady Waterford's husband and fairly bristled, it might be said, with coloured designs from her brush....

About Author

Henry James OM (15 April 1843 – 28 February 1916) was an American-British author regarded as a key transitional figure between literary realism and literary modernism, and is considered by many to be among the greatest novelists in the English language. He was the son of Henry James Sr. and the brother of renowned philosopher and psychologist William James and diarist Alice James.

He is best known for a number of novels dealing with the social and marital interplay between émigré Americans, English people, and continental Europeans. Examples of such novels include The Portrait of a Lady, The Ambassadors, and The Wings of the Dove. His later works were increasingly experimental. In describing the internal states of mind and social dynamics of his characters, James often made use of a style in which ambiguous or contradictory motives and impressions were overlaid or juxtaposed in the discussion of a character's psyche. For their unique ambiguity, as well as for other aspects of their composition, his late works have been compared to impressionist painting.

His novella The Turn of the Screw has garnered a reputation as the most analysed and ambiguous ghost story in the English language and remains his most widely adapted work in other media. He also wrote a number of other highly regarded ghost stories and is considered one of the greatest masters of the field.

James published articles and books of criticism, travel, biography, autobiography, and plays. Born in the United States, James largely relocated to Europe as a young man and eventually settled in England, becoming a British subject in 1915, one year before his death. James was nominated for the Nobel Prize in Literature in 1911, 1912 and 1916.

Life

Early years, 1843–1883

James was born at 2 Washington Place in New York City on 15 April 1843. His parents were Mary Walsh and Henry James Sr. His father was intelligent and steadfastly congenial. He was a lecturer and philosopher who had inherited independent means from his father, an Albany banker and investor. Mary came from a wealthy family long settled in New York City. Her sister Katherine lived with her adult family for an extended period of time. Henry Jr. had three brothers, William, who was one year his senior, and younger brothers Wilkinson (Wilkie) and Robertson. His younger sister was Alice. Both of his parents were of Irish and Scottish descent.

The family first lived in Albany, at 70 N. Pearl St., and then moved to Fourteenth Street in New York City when James was still a young boy. His education was calculated by his father to expose him to many influences, primarily scientific and philosophical; it was described by Percy Lubbock, the editor of his selected letters, as "extraordinarily haphazard and promiscuous." James did not share the usual education in Latin and Greek classics. Between 1855 and 1860, the James' household traveled to London, Paris, Geneva, Boulogne-sur-Mer and Newport, Rhode Island, according to the father's current interests and publishing ventures, retreating to the United States when funds were low. Henry studied primarily with tutors and briefly attended schools while the family traveled in Europe. Their longest stays were in France, where Henry began to feel at home and became fluent in French. He was afflicted with a stutter, which seems to have manifested itself only when he spoke English; in French, he did not stutter.

In 1860 the family returned to Newport. There Henry became a friend of the painter John La Farge, who introduced him to French literature, and in particular, to Balzac. James later called Balzac his "greatest master," and said that he had learned more about the craft of fiction from him than from anyone else.

In the autumn of 1861 Henry received an injury, probably to his back, while fighting a fire. This injury, which resurfaced at times throughout his life, made him unfit for military service in the American Civil War.

In 1864 the James family moved to Boston, Massachusetts to be near William, who had enrolled first in the Lawrence Scientific School at Harvard and then in the medical school. In 1862 Henry attended Harvard Law School, but realised that he was not interested in studying law. He pursued his interest in literature and associated with authors and critics William Dean Howells and Charles Eliot Norton in Boston and Cambridge, formed lifelong friendships with Oliver Wendell Holmes Jr., the future Supreme Court Justice, and with James and Annie Fields, his first professional mentors.

His first published work was a review of a stage performance, "Miss Maggie Mitchell in Fanchon the Cricket," published in 1863. About a year later, A Tragedy of Error, his first short story, was published anonymously. James's first payment was for an appreciation of Sir Walter Scott's novels, written for the North American Review. He wrote fiction and non-fiction pieces for The Nation and Atlantic Monthly, where Fields was editor. In 1871 he published his first novel, Watch and Ward, in serial form in the Atlantic Monthly. The novel was later published in book form in 1878.

During a 14-month trip through Europe in 1869–70 he met Ruskin, Dickens, Matthew Arnold, William Morris, and George Eliot. Rome impressed him profoundly. "Here I am then in the Eternal City," he wrote to his brother William. "At last—for the first time—I live!" He attempted to support himself as a freelance writer in Rome, then secured a position as Paris correspondent for the New York Tribune, through the influence of its editor John Hay. When these efforts failed he returned to New York City. During 1874 and 1875 he published Transatlantic Sketches, A Passionate Pilgrim, and Roderick Hudson. During this early period in his career he was influenced by Nathaniel Hawthorne.

In 1869 he settled in London. There he established relationships with Macmillan and other publishers, who paid for serial installments that they would later publish in book form. The audience for these serialized novels was largely made up of middle-class women, and James struggled to fashion serious literary work within the strictures imposed by editors' and publishers' notions of what was suitable for young women to read. He lived in rented rooms but was able to join gentlemen's clubs that had libraries and where he could entertain male friends. He was introduced to English society by Henry Adams and Charles Milnes Gaskell, the latter introducing him to the Travellers' and the Reform Clubs.

In the fall of 1875 he moved to the Latin Quarter of Paris. Aside from two trips to America, he spent the next three decades—the rest of his life—in Europe. In Paris he met Zola, Alphonse Daudet, Maupassant, Turgenev, and others. He stayed in Paris only a year before moving to London.

In England he met the leading figures of politics and culture. He continued to be a prolific writer, producing The American (1877), The Europeans (1878), a revision of Watch and Ward (1878), French Poets and Novelists (1878), Hawthorne (1879), and several shorter works of fiction. In 1878 Daisy Miller established his fame on both sides of the Atlantic. It drew notice perhaps mostly because it depicted a woman whose behavior is outside the social norms of Europe. He also began his first masterpiece, The Portrait of a Lady, which would appear in 1881.

In 1877 he first visited Wenlock Abbey in Shropshire, home of his friend Charles Milnes Gaskell whom he had met through Henry Adams. He was much inspired by the darkly romantic Abbey and the surrounding countryside, which features in his essay Abbeys and Castles. In particular the gloomy monastic fishponds behind the Abbey are said to have inspired the lake in The Turn of the Screw.

While living in London, James continued to follow the careers of the "French realists", Émile Zola in particular. Their stylistic methods influenced his own work in the years to come. Hawthorne's influence on him faded during this period, replaced by George Eliot and Ivan Turgenev. 1879–1882 saw the publication of The Europeans, Washington Square, Confidence, and The Portrait of a Lady. He visited America in 1882–1883, then returned to London.

The period from 1881 to 1883 was marked by several losses. His mother died in 1881, followed by his father a few months later, and then by his brother Wilkie. Emerson, an old family friend, died in 1882. His friend Turgenev died in 1883.

Middle years, 1884–1897

In 1884 James made another visit to Paris. There he met again with Zola, Daudet, and Goncourt. He had been following the careers of the French "realist" or "naturalist" writers, and was increasingly influenced by them. In 1886, he published The Bostonians and The Princess Casamassima, both influenced by the French writers he'd studied assiduously. Critical reaction and sales were poor. He wrote to Howells that the books had hurt his career rather than helped because they had "reduced the desire, and demand, for my productions to zero". During this time he became friends with Robert Louis Stevenson, John Singer Sargent, Edmund Gosse, George du Maurier, Paul Bourget, and Constance Fenimore Woolson. His third novel from the 1880s was The Tragic Muse. Although he was following the precepts of Zola in his novels of the '80s, their tone and attitude are closer to the fiction of Alphonse Daudet. The lack of critical and financial success for his novels during this period led him to try writing for the theatre. (His dramatic works and his experiences with theatre are discussed below.)

In the last quarter of 1889, he started translating "for pure and copious lucre" Port Tarascon, the third volume of Alphonse Daudet adventures of Tartarin de Tarascon. Serialized in Harper's Monthly Magazine from June 1890, this translation praised as "clever" by The Spectator was published in January 1891 by Sampson Low, Marston, Searle & Rivington.

After the stage failure of Guy Domville in 1895, James was near despair and thoughts of death plagued him. The years spent on dramatic works were not entirely a loss. As he moved into the last phase of his career he found ways to adapt dramatic techniques into the novel form.

In the late 1880s and throughout the 1890s James made several trips through Europe. He spent a long stay in Italy in 1887. In that year the short novel The Aspern Papers and The Reverberator were published.

Late years, 1898–1916

In 1897–1898 he moved to Rye, Sussex, and wrote The Turn of the Screw. 1899–1900 saw the publication of The Awkward Age and The Sacred

Fount. During 1902–1904 he wrote The Ambassadors, The Wings of the Dove, and The Golden Bowl.

In 1904 he revisited America and lectured on Balzac. In 1906–1910 he published The American Scene and edited the "New York Edition", a 24-volume collection of his works. In 1910 his brother William died; Henry had just joined William from an unsuccessful search for relief in Europe on what then turned out to be his (Henry's) last visit to the United States (from summer 1910 to July 1911), and was near him, according to a letter he wrote, when he died.

In 1913 he wrote his autobiographies, A Small Boy and Others, and Notes of a Son and Brother. After the outbreak of the First World War in 1914 he did war work. In 1915 he became a British subject and was awarded the Order of Merit the following year. He died on 28 February 1916, in Chelsea, London. As he requested, his ashes were buried in Cambridge Cemetery in Massachusetts.

Biographers

James regularly rejected suggestions that he should marry, and after settling in London proclaimed himself "a bachelor". F. W. Dupee, in several volumes on the James family, originated the theory that he had been in love with his cousin Mary ("Minnie") Temple, but that a neurotic fear of sex kept him from admitting such affections: "James's invalidism ... was itself the symptom of some fear of or scruple against sexual love on his part." Dupee used an episode from James's memoir A Small Boy and Others, recounting a dream of a Napoleonic image in the Louvre, to exemplify James's romanticism about Europe, a Napoleonic fantasy into which he fled.

Dupee had not had access to the James family papers and worked principally from James's published memoir of his older brother, William, and the limited collection of letters edited by Percy Lubbock, heavily weighted toward James's last years. His account therefore moved directly from James's childhood, when he trailed after his older brother, to elderly invalidism. As more material became available to scholars, including the diaries of contemporaries and hundreds of affectionate and sometimes erotic letters written by James to younger men, the picture of neurotic celibacy gave way to a portrait of a closeted homosexual.

Between 1953 and 1972, Leon Edel authored a major five-volume biography of James, which accessed unpublished letters and documents after Edel gained the permission of James's family. Edel's portrayal of James included the suggestion he was celibate. It was a view first propounded by critic Saul Rosenzweig in 1943. In 1996 Sheldon M. Novick published Henry James: The Young Master, followed by Henry James: The Mature Master (2007). The first book "caused something of an uproar in Jamesian circles" as it challenged the previous received notion of celibacy, a once-familiar paradigm in biographies of homosexuals when direct evidence was non-existent. Novick also criticised Edel for following the discounted Freudian interpretation of homosexuality "as a kind of failure." The difference of opinion erupted in a series of exchanges between Edel and Novick which were published by the online magazine Slate, with the latter arguing that even the suggestion of celibacy went against James's own injunction "live!"—not "fantasize!"

A letter James wrote in old age to Hugh Walpole has been cited as an explicit statement of this. Walpole confessed to him of indulging in "high jinks", and James wrote a reply endorsing it: "We must know, as much as possible, in our beautiful art, yours & mine, what we are talking about — & the only way to know it is to have lived & loved & cursed & floundered & enjoyed & suffered — I don't think I regret a single 'excess' of my responsive youth".

The interpretation of James as living a less austere emotional life has been subsequently explored by other scholars. The often intense politics of Jamesian scholarship has also been the subject of studies. Author Colm Tóibín has said that Eve Kosofsky Sedgwick's Epistemology of the Closet made a landmark difference to Jamesian scholarship by arguing that he be read as a homosexual writer whose desire to keep his sexuality a secret shaped his layered style and dramatic artistry. According to Tóibín such a reading "removed James from the realm of dead white males who wrote about posh people. He became our contemporary."

James's letters to expatriate American sculptor Hendrik Christian Andersen have attracted particular attention. James met the 27-year-old Andersen in Rome in 1899, when James was 56, and wrote letters to Andersen that are intensely emotional: "I hold you, dearest boy, in my innermost love, & count on your feeling me—in every throb of your soul". In a letter of 6 May 1904, to his brother William, James referred to himself as "always your hopelessly celibate even though sexagenarian Henry". How accurate that description might have been is the subject of contention among James's biographers,   but the letters to Andersen were occasionally quasi-erotic: "I put, my dear boy, my arm around you, & feel the pulsation, thereby, as it were, of our excellent future & your admirable endowment." To his homosexual friend Howard Sturgis, James could write: "I repeat, almost to indiscretion, that I could live with you. Meanwhile I can only try to live without you."

His numerous letters to the many young gay men among his close male friends are more forthcoming. In a letter to Howard Sturgis, following a long visit, James refers jocularly to their "happy little congress of two" and in letters to Hugh Walpole he pursues convoluted jokes and puns about their relationship, referring to himself as an elephant who "paws you oh so benevolently" and winds about Walpole his "well meaning old trunk". His letters to Walter Berry printed by the Black Sun Press have long been celebrated for their lightly veiled eroticism.

He corresponded in almost equally extravagant language with his many female friends, writing, for example, to fellow novelist Lucy Clifford: "Dearest Lucy! What shall I say? when I love you so very, very much, and see you nine times for once that I see Others! Therefore I think that—if you want it made clear to the meanest intelligence—I love you more than I love Others." To his New York friend Mary Cadwalader Jones: "Dearest Mary Cadwalader. I yearn over you, but I yearn in vain; & your long silence really breaks my heart, mystifies, depresses, almost alarms me, to the point even of making me wonder if poor unconscious & doting old Célimare [Jones's pet name for James] has 'done' anything, in some dark somnambulism of the spirit, which has ... given you a bad moment, or a wrong impression, or a 'colourable pretext' ... However these things may be, he loves you as tenderly as ever;

nothing, to the end of time, will ever detach him from you, & he remembers those Eleventh St. matutinal intimes hours, those telephonic matinées, as the most romantic of his life ..." His long friendship with American novelist Constance Fenimore Woolson, in whose house he lived for a number of weeks in Italy in 1887, and his shock and grief over her suicide in 1894, are discussed in detail in Edel's biography and play a central role in a study by Lyndall Gordon. (Edel conjectured that Woolson was in love with James and killed herself in part because of his coldness, but Woolson's biographers have objected to Edel's account.)

Works

Style and themes

James is one of the major figures of trans-Atlantic literature. His works frequently juxtapose characters from the Old World (Europe), embodying a feudal civilisation that is beautiful, often corrupt, and alluring, and from the New World (United States), where people are often brash, open, and assertive and embody the virtues—freedom and a more highly evolved moral character—of the new American society. James explores this clash of personalities and cultures, in stories of personal relationships in which power is exercised well or badly. His protagonists were often young American women facing oppression or abuse, and as his secretary Theodora Bosanquet remarked in her monograph Henry James at Work:

> When he walked out of the refuge of his study and into the world and looked around him, he saw a place of torment, where creatures of prey perpetually thrust their claws into the quivering flesh of doomed, defenseless children of light ... His novels are a repeated exposure of this wickedness, a reiterated and passionate plea for the fullest freedom of development, unimperiled by reckless and barbarous stupidity.

Critics have jokingly described three phases in the development of James's prose: "James I, James II, and The Old Pretender." He wrote short stories and plays. Finally, in his third and last period he returned to the long, serialised novel. Beginning in the second period, but most noticeably in the third, he increasingly abandoned direct statement in favour of frequent double negatives, and complex descriptive imagery. Single paragraphs began to run for page after page, in which an initial noun would be succeeded by pronouns surrounded by clouds of adjectives and prepositional clauses, far from their original referents, and verbs would be deferred and then preceded by a series of adverbs. The overall effect could be a vivid evocation of a scene as perceived by a sensitive observer. It has been debated whether this change of style was engendered by James's shifting from writing to dictating to a typist, a change made during the composition of What Maisie Knew.

In its intense focus on the consciousness of his major characters, James's later work foreshadows extensive developments in 20th century fiction. Indeed, he might have influenced stream-of-consciousness writers such as Virginia Woolf, who not only read some of his novels but also wrote essays about them. Both contemporary and modern readers have found the late style difficult and unnecessary; his friend Edith Wharton, who admired him greatly, said that there were passages in his work that were all but incomprehensible. James was harshly portrayed by H. G. Wells as a hippopotamus laboriously attempting to pick up a pea that had got into a corner of its cage. The "late James" style was ably parodied by Max Beerbohm in "The Mote in the Middle Distance".

More important for his work overall may have been his position as an expatriate, and in other ways an outsider, living in Europe. While he came from middle-class and provincial beginnings (seen from the perspective of European polite society) he worked very hard to gain access to all levels of society, and the settings of his fiction range from working class to aristocratic, and often describe the efforts of middle-class Americans to make their way in European capitals. He confessed he got some of his best story ideas from gossip at the dinner table or at country house weekends. He worked for a living, however, and lacked the experiences of select schools, university, and army service, the common bonds of masculine society. He was furthermore a man whose tastes and interests were, according to the prevailing standards of Victorian era Anglo-American culture, rather feminine, and who was shadowed by the cloud of prejudice that then and later accompanied suspicions of his homosexuality. Edmund Wilson famously compared James's objectivity to Shakespeare's:

One would be in a position to appreciate James better if one compared him with the dramatists of the seventeenth century—Racine and Molière, whom he resembles in form as well as in point of view, and even Shakespeare, when allowances are made for the most extreme differences in subject and form. These poets are not, like Dickens and Hardy, writers of melodrama—either humorous or pessimistic, nor secretaries of society like Balzac, nor prophets like Tolstoy: they are occupied simply with the presentation of conflicts of moral character, which they do not concern themselves about softening or averting. They do not indict society for these situations: they regard them as universal and inevitable. They do not even blame God for allowing them: they accept them as the conditions of life.

It is also possible to see many of James's stories as psychological thought-experiments. In his preface to the New York edition of The American he describes the development of the story in his mind as exactly such: the "situation" of an American, "some robust but insidiously beguiled and betrayed, some cruelly wronged, compatriot..." with the focus of the story being on the response of this wronged man. The Portrait of a Lady may be an experiment to see what happens when an idealistic young woman suddenly becomes very rich. In many of his tales, characters seem to exemplify alternative futures and possibilities, as most markedly in "The Jolly Corner", in which the protagonist and a ghost-doppelganger live alternative American and European lives; and in others, like The Ambassadors, an older James seems fondly to regard his own younger self facing a crucial moment.

Major novels

The first period of James's fiction, usually considered to have culminated in The Portrait of a Lady, concentrated on the contrast between Europe and America. The style of these novels is generally straightforward and, though personally characteristic, well within the norms of 19th-century fiction. Roderick Hudson (1875) is a Künstlerroman that traces the development of the title character, an extremely talented sculptor. Although the book shows some signs of immaturity—this was James's first serious attempt at a full-length novel—it has attracted favourable comment due to the vivid realisation of the three major characters: Roderick Hudson, superbly gifted but unstable and unreliable; Rowland Mallet, Roderick's limited but much more mature friend and patron; and Christina Light, one of James's most enchanting and maddening femmes fatales. The pair of Hudson and Mallet has been seen as representing the two sides of James's own nature: the wildly imaginative artist and the brooding conscientious mentor.

In The Portrait of a Lady (1881) James concluded the first phase of his career with a novel that remains his most popular piece of long fiction. The story is of a spirited young American woman, Isabel Archer, who "affronts her destiny" and finds it overwhelming. She inherits a large amount of money and subsequently becomes the victim of Machiavellian scheming by two American expatriates. The narrative is set mainly in Europe, especially in England and Italy. Generally regarded as the masterpiece of his early phase, The Portrait of a Lady is described as a psychological novel, exploring the minds of his characters, and almost a work of social science, exploring the differences between Europeans and Americans, the old and the new worlds.

The second period of James's career, which extends from the publication of The Portrait of a Lady through the end of the nineteenth century, features less popular novels including The Princess Casamassima, published serially in The Atlantic Monthly in 1885–1886, and The Bostonians, published serially in The Century Magazine during the same period. This period also featured James's celebrated Gothic novella, The Turn of the Screw.

The third period of James's career reached its most significant achievement in three novels published just around the start of the 20th century: The Wings of the Dove (1902), The Ambassadors (1903), and The Golden Bowl (1904). Critic F. O. Matthiessen called this "trilogy" James's major phase, and these novels have certainly received intense critical study. It was the second-written of the books, The Wings of the Dove (1902) that was the first published because it attracted no serialization. This novel tells the story of Milly Theale, an American heiress stricken with a serious disease, and her impact on the people around her. Some of these people befriend Milly with honourable motives, while others are more self-interested. James stated in his autobiographical books that Milly was based on Minny Temple, his beloved cousin who died at an early age of tuberculosis. He said that he attempted in the novel to wrap her memory in the "beauty and dignity of art".

Shorter narratives

James was particularly interested in what he called the "beautiful and blest nouvelle", or the longer form of short narrative. Still, he produced a number of very short stories in which he achieved notable compression of sometimes complex subjects. The following narratives are representative of James's achievement in the shorter forms of fiction.

- "A Tragedy of Error" (1864), short story
- "The Story of a Year" (1865), short story
- A Passionate Pilgrim (1871), novella
- Madame de Mauves (1874), novella
- Daisy Miller (1878), novella
- The Aspern Papers (1888), novella
- The Lesson of the Master (1888), novella
- The Pupil (1891), short story
- "The Figure in the Carpet" (1896), short story
- The Beast in the Jungle (1903), novella
- An International Episode (1878)
- Picture and Text
- Four Meetings (1885)
- A London Life, and Other Tales (1889)
- The Spoils of Poynton (1896)

- Embarrassments (1896)
- The Two Magics: The Turn of the Screw, Covering End (1898)
- A Little Tour of France (1900)
- The Sacred Fount (1901)
- Views and Reviews (1908)
- The Wings of the Dove, Volume I (1902)
- The Wings of the Dove, Volume II (1909)
- The Finer Grain (1910)
- The Outcry (1911)
- Lady Barbarina: The Siege of London, An International Episode and Other Tales (1922)
- The Birthplace (1922)

Plays

At several points in his career James wrote plays, beginning with one-act plays written for periodicals in 1869 and 1871 and a dramatisation of his popular novella Daisy Miller in 1882. From 1890 to 1892, having received a bequest that freed him from magazine publication, he made a strenuous effort to succeed on the London stage, writing a half-dozen plays of which only one, a dramatisation of his novel The American, was produced. This play was performed for several years by a touring repertory company and had a respectable run in London, but did not earn very much money for James. His other plays written at this time were not produced.

In 1893, however, he responded to a request from actor-manager George Alexander for a serious play for the opening of his renovated St. James's Theatre, and wrote a long drama, Guy Domville, which Alexander produced. There was a noisy uproar on the opening night, 5 January 1895, with hissing from the gallery when James took his bow after the final curtain, and the author was upset. The play received moderately good reviews and had a modest run of four weeks before being taken off to make way for Oscar Wilde's The Importance of Being Earnest, which Alexander thought would have better prospects for the coming season.

After the stresses and disappointment of these efforts James insisted that he would write no more for the theatre, but within weeks had agreed to write a curtain-raiser for Ellen Terry. This became the one-act "Summersoft", which he later rewrote into a short story, "Covering End", and then expanded into a full-length play, The High Bid, which had a brief run in London in 1907, when James made another concerted effort to write for the stage. He wrote three new plays, two of which were in production when the death of Edward VII on 6 May 1910 plunged London into mourning and theatres closed. Discouraged by failing health and the stresses of theatrical work, James did not renew his efforts in the theatre, but recycled his plays as successful novels. The Outcry was a best-seller in the United States when it was published in 1911. During the years 1890–1893 when he was most engaged with the theatre, James wrote a good deal of theatrical criticism and assisted Elizabeth Robins and others in translating and producing Henrik Ibsen for the first time in London.

Leon Edel argued in his psychoanalytic biography that James was traumatised by the opening night uproar that greeted Guy Domville, and that it plunged him into a prolonged depression. The successful later novels, in Edel's view, were the result of a kind of self-analysis, expressed in fiction, which partly freed him from his fears. Other biographers and scholars have not accepted this account, however; the more common view being that of F.O. Matthiessen, who wrote: "Instead of being crushed by the collapse of his hopes [for the theatre]... he felt a resurgence of new energy."

Non-fiction

Beyond his fiction, James was one of the more important literary critics in the history of the novel. In his classic essay The Art of Fiction (1884), he argued against rigid prescriptions on the novelist's choice of subject and method of treatment. He maintained that the widest possible freedom in content and approach would help ensure narrative fiction's continued vitality.

James wrote many valuable critical articles on other novelists; typical is his book-length study of Nathaniel Hawthorne, which has been the subject of critical debate. Richard Brodhead has suggested that the study was emblematic of James's struggle with Hawthorne's influence, and constituted an effort to place the elder writer "at a disadvantage." Gordon Fraser, meanwhile, has suggested that the study was part of a more commercial effort by James to introduce himself to British readers as Hawthorne's natural successor.

When James assembled the New York Edition of his fiction in his final years, he wrote a series of prefaces that subjected his own work to searching, occasionally harsh criticism.

At 22 James wrote The Noble School of Fiction for The Nation's first issue in 1865. He would write, in all, over 200 essays and book, art, and theatre reviews for the magazine.

For most of his life James harboured ambitions for success as a playwright. He converted his novel The American into a play that enjoyed modest returns in the early 1890s. In all he wrote about a dozen plays, most of which went unproduced. His costume drama Guy Domville failed disastrously on its opening night in 1895. James then largely abandoned his efforts to conquer the stage and returned to his fiction. In his Notebooks he maintained that his theatrical experiment benefited his novels and tales by helping him dramatise his characters' thoughts and emotions. James produced a small but valuable amount of theatrical criticism, including perceptive appreciations of Henrik Ibsen.

With his wide-ranging artistic interests, James occasionally wrote on the visual arts. Perhaps his most valuable contribution was his favourable assessment of fellow expatriate John Singer Sargent, a painter whose critical status has improved markedly in recent decades. James also wrote sometimes charming, sometimes brooding articles about various places he visited and lived in. His most famous books of travel writing include Italian Hours (an example of the charming approach) and The American Scene (most definitely on the brooding side).

James was one of the great letter-writers of any era. More than ten thousand of his personal letters are extant, and over three thousand have been published in a large number of collections. A complete edition of James's letters began publication in 2006, edited by Pierre Walker and Greg Zacharias. As of 2014, eight volumes have been published, covering the period from 1855 to 1880. James's correspondents included celebrated contemporaries like Robert Louis Stevenson, Edith Wharton and Joseph Conrad, along with many others in his wide circle of friends and acquaintances. The letters range from the "mere twaddle of graciousness" to serious discussions of artistic, social and personal issues.

Very late in life James began a series of autobiographical works: A Small Boy and Others, Notes of a Son and Brother, and the unfinished The Middle Years. These books portray the development of a classic observer who was passionately interested in artistic creation but was somewhat reticent about participating fully in the life around him.

Reception

Criticism, biographies and fictional treatments

James's work has remained steadily popular with the limited audience of educated readers to whom he spoke during his lifetime, and has remained firmly in the canon, but, after his death, some American critics, such as Van Wyck Brooks, expressed hostility towards James for his long expatriation and eventual naturalisation as a British subject. Other critics such as E. M. Forster complained about what they saw as James's squeamishness in the treatment of sex and other possibly controversial material, or dismissed his late style as difficult and obscure, relying heavily on extremely long sentences and excessively latinate language. Similarly Oscar Wilde criticised him for writing "fiction as if it were a painful duty". Vernon Parrington, composing a canon of American literature, condemned James for having cut himself off from America. Jorge Luis Borges wrote about him, "Despite the scruples and delicate complexities of James, his work suffers from a major defect: the absence of life." And Virginia Woolf, writing to Lytton Strachey, asked, "Please tell me what you find in Henry James. ... we have his works here, and

I read, and I can't find anything but faintly tinged rose water, urbane and sleek, but vulgar and pale as Walter Lamb. Is there really any sense in it?" The novelist W. Somerset Maugham wrote, "He did not know the English as an Englishman instinctively knows them and so his English characters never to my mind quite ring true," and argued "The great novelists, even in seclusion, have lived life passionately. Henry James was content to observe it from a window." Maugham nevertheless wrote, "The fact remains that those last novels of his, notwithstanding their unreality, make all other novels, except the very best, unreadable." Colm Tóibín observed that James "never really wrote about the English very well. His English characters don't work for me."

Despite these criticisms, James is now valued for his psychological and moral realism, his masterful creation of character, his low-key but playful humour, and his assured command of the language. In his 1983 book, The Novels of Henry James, Edward Wagenknecht offers an assessment that echoes Theodora Bosanquet's:

> "To be completely great," Henry James wrote in an early review, "a work of art must lift up the heart," and his own novels do this to an outstanding degree ... More than sixty years after his death, the great novelist who sometimes professed to have no opinions stands foursquare in the great Christian humanistic and democratic tradition. The men and women who, at the height of World War II, raided the secondhand shops for his out-of-print books knew what they were about. For no writer ever raised a braver banner to which all who love freedom might adhere.

William Dean Howells saw James as a representative of a new realist school of literary art which broke with the English romantic tradition epitomised by the works of Charles Dickens and William Makepeace Thackeray. Howells wrote that realism found "its chief exemplar in Mr. James... A novelist he is not, after the old fashion, or after any fashion but his own." F.R. Leavis championed Henry James as a novelist of "established pre-eminence" in The Great Tradition (1948), asserting that The Portrait of a Lady and The Bostonians were "the two most brilliant novels in the language." James is now prized as a master of point of view who moved literary fiction forward by insisting in showing, not telling, his stories to the reader. (Source: Wikipedia)

NOTABLE WORKS

NOVELS

Watch and Ward (1871)

Roderick Hudson (1875)

The American (1877)

The Europeans (1878)

Confidence (1879)

Washington Square (1880)

The Portrait of a Lady (1881)

The Bostonians (1886)

The Princess Casamassima (1886)

The Reverberator (1888)

The Tragic Muse (1890)

The Other House (1896)

The Spoils of Poynton (1897)

What Maisie Knew (1897)

The Awkward Age (1899)

The Sacred Fount (1901)

The Wings of the Dove (1902)

The Ambassadors (1903)

The Golden Bowl (1904)

The Whole Family (collaborative novel with eleven other authors, 1908)

The Outcry (1911)

The Ivory Tower (unfinished, published posthumously 1917)

The Sense of the Past (unfinished, published posthumously 1917)

SHORT STORIES AND NOVELLAS

A Tragedy of Error (1864)

The Story of a Year (1865)

A Landscape Painter (1866)

A Day of Days (1866)

My Friend Bingham (1867)

Poor Richard (1867)

The Story of a Masterpiece (1868)

A Most Extraordinary Case (1868)

A Problem (1868)

De Grey: A Romance (1868)

Osborne's Revenge (1868)

The Romance of Certain Old Clothes (1868)

A Light Man (1869)

Gabrielle de Bergerac (1869)

Travelling Companions (1870)

A Passionate Pilgrim (1871)

At Isella (1871)

Master Eustace (1871)

Guest's Confession (1872)

The Madonna of the Future (1873)

The Sweetheart of M. Briseux (1873)

The Last of the Valerii (1874)

Madame de Mauves (1874)

Adina (1874)

Professor Fargo (1874)

Eugene Pickering (1874)

Benvolio (1875)

Crawford's Consistency (1876)

The Ghostly Rental (1876)

Four Meetings (1877)

Rose-Agathe (1878, as Théodolinde)

Daisy Miller (1878)

Longstaff's Marriage (1878)

An International Episode (1878)

The Pension Beaurepas (1879)

A Diary of a Man of Fifty (1879)

A Bundle of Letters (1879)

The Point of View (1882)

The Siege of London (1883)

Impressions of a Cousin (1883)

Lady Barberina (1884)

Pandora (1884)

The Author of Beltraffio (1884)

Georgina's Reasons (1884)

A New England Winter (1884)

The Path of Duty (1884)

Mrs. Temperly (1887)

Louisa Pallant (1888)

The Aspern Papers (1888)

The Liar (1888)

The Modern Warning (1888, originally published as The Two Countries)

A London Life (1888)

The Patagonia (1888)

The Lesson of the Master (1888)

The Solution (1888)

The Pupil (1891)

Brooksmith (1891)

The Marriages (1891)

The Chaperon (1891)

Sir Edmund Orme (1891)

Nona Vincent (1892)

The Real Thing (1892)

The Private Life (1892)

Lord Beaupré (1892)

The Visits (1892)

Sir Dominick Ferrand (1892)

Greville Fane (1892)

Collaboration (1892)

Owen Wingrave (1892)

The Wheel of Time (1892)

The Middle Years (1893)

The Death of the Lion (1894)

The Coxon Fund (1894)

The Next Time (1895)

Glasses (1896)

The Altar of the Dead (1895)

The Figure in the Carpet (1896)

The Way It Came (1896, also published as The Friends of the Friends)

The Turn of the Screw (1898)

Covering End (1898)

In the Cage (1898)

John Delavoy (1898)

The Given Case (1898)

Europe (1899)

The Great Condition (1899)

The Real Right Thing (1899)

Paste (1899)

The Great Good Place (1900)

Maud-Evelyn (1900)

Miss Gunton of Poughkeepsie (1900)

The Tree of Knowledge (1900)

The Abasement of the Northmores (1900)

The Third Person (1900)

The Special Type (1900)

The Tone of Time (1900)

Broken Wings (1900)

The Two Faces (1900)

Mrs. Medwin (1901)

The Beldonald Holbein (1901)

The Story in It (1902)

Flickerbridge (1902)

The Birthplace (1903)

The Beast in the Jungle (1903)

The Papers (1903)

Fordham Castle (1904)

Julia Bride (1908)

The Jolly Corner (1908)

The Velvet Glove (1909)

Mora Montravers (1909)

Crapy Cornelia (1909)

The Bench of Desolation (1909)

A Round of Visits (1910)

OTHER

Transatlantic Sketches (1875)

French Poets and Novelists (1878)

Hawthorne (1879)

Portraits of Places (1883)

A Little Tour in France (1884)

Partial Portraits (1888)

Essays in London and Elsewhere (1893)

Picture and Text (1893)

Terminations (1893)

Theatricals (1894)

Theatricals: Second Series (1895)

Guy Domville (1895)

The Soft Side (1900)

William Wetmore Story and His Friends (1903)

The Better Sort (1903)

English Hours (1905)

The Question of our Speech; The Lesson of Balzac. Two Lectures (1905)

The American Scene (1907)

Views and Reviews (1908)

Italian Hours (1909)

A Small Boy and Others (1913)

Notes on Novelists (1914)

Notes of a Son and Brother (1914)

Within the Rim (1918)

Travelling Companions (1919)

Notebooks (various, published posthumously)

The Middle Years (unfinished, published posthumously 1917)

A Most Unholy Trade (1925, published posthumously)

The Art of the Novel : Critical Prefaces (1934)